MW01516084

BLOOD MONEY

QUINN RAIDERS BOOK 2

ROBERT VAUGHAN

WOLFPACK
PUBLISHING
— EST 2013 —

Blood Money
Quinn Raiders Book 2

Paperback Edition
© Copyright 2018 by Robert Vaughan (as revised)

Wolfpack Publishing
6032 Wheat Penny Avenue
Las Vegas, NV 89122

This book is a work of fiction. Any references to historical events, real people or real places are used fictitiously. Other names, characters, places and events are products of the author's imagination, and any resemblance to actual events or places or persons living or dead is entirely coincidental.

All rights reserved. No part of this book may be reproduced by any means without the prior written consent of the publisher, other than brief quotes for reviews.

Paperback ISBN 978-1-64119-536-2
eBook ISBN 978-1-64119-535-5

Library of Congress Control Number: 2018963810

BLOOD MONEY

CHAPTER ONE

IN THE COOL SHADOW OF SAN FRANCISCO PEAK, FOUR OF Quinn's Raiders: Hank Proudy, Billy Joe Higgins, and the Depro brothers, Bob and Loomis, were in the process of breaking camp: It had been a meager camp; the coffee, tobacco, and liquor were gone, and only beans, jerky, and a little salt remained among their stores.

Their coffers hadn't always been so bare. In fact, the boys had left southern Arizona several weeks earlier with enough money to enjoy their passage through the various towns and cities along their route. But several nights of cavorting with the "soiled doves" of Tucson, a drinking bout in Phoenix, and a bad run of cards in Prescott had depleted their funds to the point that they were now without enough money even for the most modest hotel rooms. This lean time was the reason their leader, Marcus Quinn, wasn't with them.

The boys had pooled their money, then drew for the high card to see who had the luck with them. The one with luck would ride into town and find a card game; not a big one, just one that would let him win enough for a small stake that could be shared with the others.

When they cut the cards, Marcus drew a ten of hearts; not a very big card, but, considering the way everyone's luck had been running, big enough to make Marcus the one who would represent them.

They were near the town of Flagstaff. Flagstaff would be a place of some importance in northern Arizona in a short time. Not only was it the largest town in the northern part of the territory, but thanks to the planned arrival of the railroad, it was little more than a week's travel time from such places as St. Louis, Chicago, and Detroit. Merchants had flocked there, setting up shops in time for the new trade.

Flagstaff was laid out in a large X, formed by the crossing of two major streets. Santa Fe Street, which ran parallel with the railroad of the same name, was one, and the crossroad, San Francisco Street, was the other. San Francisco Street was named, not after the city in California, but after San Francisco Peak, the nearest mountain.

Santa Fe was the main street. It ran east and west, presenting a solid row of well-constructed wooden buildings: general stores, leather-goods stores, a couple of laundries, and a disproportionate number of saloons and gambling halls.

One of the more popular saloons was the Golden Lady Saloon located on Santa Fe street near the depot. The Golden Lady had brought in, at great expense, a fine crystal chandelier. It also had a bar of polished

mahogany, solid brass spittoons, a brass foot rail, and a three-by-six-foot oil painting of a nude woman reclining on a golden couch contemplating a message she held in her hand, while her nubian servant poured water into a large golden tub behind her.

The saloon drew its name from the painting, and many a cowboy had speculated about the note held in the hands of that voluptuous lady.

It was to this place that Marcus had come to play cards, and though he wasn't having a phenomenal run of luck, he had been winning steadily and now had enough that the boys could at least restock their trail supplies. He had just been called on a rather modest bet, and he laid his hand down on the table, face up.

"Looks like I win again," he said easily.

"The hell you say!"

The loud, hoarse curse had exploded from the throat of one of the poker players in Marcus's game. His outburst was followed by the crashing sound of a chair tipping over as he stood abruptly. A woman's laughter halted in midtrill, and the piano player pulled his hands away from the keyboard so that the last three notes of

"Buffalo Gals" hung raggedly, discordantly in the air. All conversation ceased, and everyone in the crowded saloon turned toward the cause of the disturbance.

A tall, lanky man with a drooping black mustache and cold, fishlike eyes stood in front of the chair he had just overturned. He pointed a long, accusing finger across the table at Marcus Quinn. The object of his anger seemed to be Marcus's winning hand. The money in the pot amounted to twelve dollars and eighty cents.

"You sonofabitch! Where did that ace come from?"

"Jensen, what are you talking about?" one of the other card players asked. "You dealt this hand, not him."

"Yeah," the other player put in. "This has been a real friendly game 'til now. ... He ain't won no more'n any of the rest of us."

"You two stay out of this unless you're fixin' to buy in for a piece of the trouble," Jensen said. He looked at Marcus again. "Now, I'm askin' you a second time. Where'd you get that ace?"

The saloon was deathly quiet now as everyone strained to hear every word spoken. The large clock standing against the wall by the coat rack, and which normally marked the passage of the day unnoticed, now seemed to proclaim each syllable of time loudly. More than one of the customers, sensing that something momentous was about to happen, checked his own pocket watch against the clock, the better to fix the time in their minds so that every detail would be accurate for the later telling.

"You dealt it to me from the bottom of the deck," Marcus said quietly.

Jensen snorted what might have been a sarcastic laugh. "Now, why would I want to do a fool thing like that?" he asked.

"I was wonderin' the same thing," Marcus said. "Then I figured you was either bein' nice to me, or tryin' to set me up for a killin'."

Jensen smiled. "Well, now, ain't you the smart one?" He moved his hand toward the pistol at his side. "Reckon you're just gonna have to draw."

"Jensen, that ain't no fair fight," someone said. "This here feller's sittin' down, an' you're a-standin' up."

"No, I don't reckon it is fair," Jensen agreed. "But this is the way of it." His smile grew broader, and his hand hovered over his pistol. "Now, mister, I told you to pull your gun."

As yet, Marcus had made no move toward his own gun, nor even to improve his own position. But he did smile up at the tall man, and his smile was even colder and more frightening than Jensen's.

"Since you already agreed this ain't no fair fight, Jensen, maybe I ought to tell you I already got my gun in my hand under the table."

"Mister, who you trying to kid?" Jensen asked. "You're gun's in your holster ... I can see it."

"What I got in my hand is a holdout gun," Marcus

said. "A derringer, two barrels, forty-one caliber. I can put a hole in your chest big enough to stick my fist into."

"You're bluffin'."

"Try me."

Jensen stood for a moment longer, trying to decide whether or not he would call Marcus's bluff. His eyes narrowed, a muscle in his cheek twitched, and perspiration beads broke out on his forehead.

"All right," he finally said. "Only this ain't gonna stop here. I'm callin' you out, mister. I'm goin' out in the street to wait for you. You got thirty seconds to come out, or I'm cornin' back in after you."

The crowd in the saloon watched Jensen leave, saw the bat-wing doors swing closed in his wake, then they looked back toward Marcus. Marcus still held his right hand under the table, then he brought it up and everyone saw that he wasn't holding a derringer as he had claimed, but a cigar. He put the cigar in his mouth, smiled broadly, lit it, and took a puff. Marcus had just run a monumental bluff, and they had all seen it.

"Are you goin' out there, mister?" one of the men asked.

"Don't reckon I got much choice," Marcus said. He pulled his pistol and checked the loads in his chamber, then slipped the pistol back into his holster. "If I don't face him head up, like as not he'll shoot me in the back."

In a town like Flagstaff, news of an impending gunfight seemed to travel faster than the telegraph.

Santa Fe Avenue, which had been busy with commerce just a moment earlier, had suddenly become deserted, except for Jensen who stood in the middle of the street about one hundred feet away. Men and women scurried down the sidewalks, stepping into buildings to get out of the line of fire, while taking up an observer's position in the doors and windows so they would miss nothing. Even the horses had been moved off the street as nervous owners feared they might get hit by a stray bullet. Only Marcus's horse remained tied to the hitching post in front of the saloon. He whickered and stamped his foot nervously as if sensing that something was happening.

Jensen moved his hand just over his pistol.

"Well, now, where's your belly gun?" Jensen called.

"Won't be needin' it," Marcus answered.

Suddenly, a bullet fried the air just beside his ear, hit the dirt beside him, then skipped off with a high-pitched whine on down the street. The sound of the rifle shot reached him at about the same time, and Marcus dropped and rolled to his left, his gun already in his hand. That was when he saw the rifleman standing on the porch roof of the general store just behind the Watterman's Finest Selections sign. The would-be assailant was operating the lever, chambering in another round, when Marcus fired. Marcus's shot flew true, and he saw the rifle drop to the ground as the ambusher grabbed his throat, then pitched forward, turning a half-flip in the air to land flat on his back, sending up a little puff of dust from the impact of his falling body.

By now Jensen had his own pistol out and fired, but Marcus, with the instinct of survival, had rolled to his right after his first shot. As a result Jensen's bullet crashed harmlessly into the wooden front stoop of the Delmonte Cafe. A woman inside screamed with fear as she realized how close the bullet had come to what she had assumed would be a safe vantage point.

From a prone position on the ground, Marcus fired at Jensen and hit him in the knee. Jensen let out a howl and went down. He was still firing, and Marcus felt a bullet tear through the crown of his hat.

Now a third party entered the fray as someone raised up from behind the watering trough in front of the Chinese laundry and fired at Marcus. More hesitant than the other two, this third gunman was less skilled with a pistol. Marcus could see that he was holding the pistol up and jerking the trigger, pulling the gun off target. Marcus decided to take care of Jensen first.

At the campsite just out of town, Hank was the first one to hear the shooting.

"You boys hear that?" he asked.

"Yeah, shooting," Bob said. "You think it's Marcus?"

"I think we damn sure better find out," Hank replied, swinging into his saddle. All four were mounted instantly, and before the second volley of shots were fired, they were riding at a full gallop toward the town to the sound of the firing.

Marcus threw another shot toward Jensen. But Jensen was lying in the road now, and he made a more difficult target.

"McPheeters!" Jensen called. "McPheeters, can you get him?"

"I'm tryin'!" the man behind the watering trough answered. He raised up and fired again, and this time his bullet came close enough that Marcus could hear it as it whined by.

Marcus was lying out in the open, so he got up and ran across the street, bending low and firing as he went. He dived behind the porch of the barbershop, then rose and saw that he had a perfect shot at McPheeters. He fired, saw McPheeters drop his pistol in the watering trough, then fall back with blood oozing out of the bullet hole in the side of his chest.

By now Jensen had managed to improve his own position, and he fired again at Marcus. His bullet sent splinters of wood into Marcus's face, and Marcus put his hand up then pulled it away peppered with his own blood.

"A hunnert dollars!" Jensen shouted to anyone on the street who would listen. "I'll give a hunnert dollars to any man that helps me kill this sonofabitch!"

Marcus stared across the street, trying to find an opening for a shot. Then he smiled. Jensen had improved his position by getting out of the street and behind a wooden bench in front of a dressmaker's shop. What he didn't realize though, was that the large mirror in the window of the dressmaker's shop showed his reflection, and from across the street, Marcus watched as Jensen inched along on his belly to the far end of the bench. Marcus took slow and deliberate aim at the end of the bench where he knew Jensen's face would appear.

Slowly Jensen peered around the corner of the bench to see where Marcus was and what was going on. Marcus cocked his pistol and waited. When enough of Jensen's head was exposed to give him a target, Marcus squeezed the trigger. The Colt .44 roared and bucked in his hand. A cloud of smoke billowed up then floated away. When the cloud cleared, Marcus saw Jensen lying face down in the dirt with a pool of blood spreading out from under his head.

Marcus heard the hoof beats of running horses, and he swung his gun toward the west end of the street, ready, if need be, to take on some more. But when he saw the four riders who were coming toward, he smiled in relief, then stood up and slipped his pistol back into his holster. The riders dismounted, drew their own weapons, and looked around with experi-enced eyes to search roofs and the corners of buildings for any additional adversaries. If there were any, they'd be afraid to make their play now against the full force of the outlaw band, Quinn's Raiders.

Marcus was the leader of the group since he'd been

their captain when they fought as Confederate guerrillas during the Civil War. The sergeant of the group had been Hank Proudy. He was still second-in-charge, and it was he who led the other three men into town when they heard shooting and surmised correctly that it probably involved their leader.

"You all right, Marcus?" Hank asked.

"Yeah," Marcus answered. He smiled. "If there's anyone else got a hankerin' after me, you boys scared 'em off."

"Marcus . . . this here one's still alive," Bob Depro said from the front of the Chinese laundry. Marcus and his group went down to see the wounded gunman. By now the townspeople had come out of the stores and buildings to tentatively reclaim the street they had abandoned to flying bullets moments before.

"Mister," Marcus said to the wounded gunman. "Why'd you fellas push this fight?"

"It were Jensen's doin'," the man said. He coughed and flecks of blood foamed from his mouth. Marcus knew then that he had a bullet in the lung. He wouldn't last long.

"You know Jensen?" Hank asked.

"Never saw him before I played cards with him."

"Piss him off?"

"No, I don't think so," Marcus said. "Oh, he picked a fight over the game, said I was cheatin'. But he give me the ace hisself, had it on the bottom of the deck and slipped it to me. Couldn't figure that out. Hell, there weren't more'n four or five dollars in any hand we played . . . not enough to take a chance on gettin' yourself kilt over."

The wounded gunman tried to laugh and erupted into another coughing fit.

"Don't you know?" he said. "The card game got nothin' to do with it. They's dodgers out on you men."

"Dodgers?" Billy Joe asked. "Where from?"

"Down south of the territory. You men is wanted pretty bad down there. Look in my coat pocket." Marcus reached into the man's coat pocket and pulled out a circular. He opened it up, then showed it to the others.

WANTED DEAD OR ALIVE
"QUINN'S RAIDERS"

MARCUS QUINN
HANK PROUDY
BOB DEPRO
LOOMIS DEPRO
BILLY JOE HIGGINS
$5,000 Reward
These men are armed and dangerous. They have
committed murder,
armed robbery, and cattle rustling.

The paper had been put out by the sheriff's office in Tucson, and it contained a good description of each of the boys.

"Marcus," Hank said, noticing then that the sheriff was coming across the street toward them.

Marcus folded the paper and slipped it into his pocket, then tensed as the sheriff approached. He looked at the others and saw that they were ready for anything.

"Mister," the sheriff said to Marcus. "The folks over in the saloon told me what happened, how Jensen goaded you into this fight, so I reckon I got nothin' to charge you with."

"I reckon not," Marcus answered.

The sheriff scratched his head and looked down at the gunman at their feet. "I see you kilt all three," the sheriff said.

Until that moment, Marcus didn't know this one had died, but when he looked down, he saw the man's eyes open and sightless, his mouth and chin spotted with blood.

"Didn't have no choice," Marcus said.

"Yeah, well, I don't have no choice, neither. I'm gonna have to ask you to move on outta my town. I don't want nobody around that could take out three men like you done."

"You gonna run 'im out if he don't want to go?" Hank asked with a sardonic smile.

The sheriff cleared his throat, then stroked his chin. "I reckon I'm gonna have to give it a try," he said.

Marcus chuckled. "You don't have to, Sheriff," he said. "I ain't plannin' on stayin' around here."

"Good," the sheriff mumbled.

"Got 'ny idea where we're a-goin'?" Bob asked as they crossed the street to get Marcus's horse from the hitching rail.

"Them circulars come from the south, so let's head north," Marcus said. "Arizona's done got too small for us."

As the five men rode out of town, the citizens of Flagstaff stood in awed bunches on the sidewalk and crowded down to the edge of the street to get a closer look at the man who had bested three men in a desperate gunfight. A boy, about ten, drifted out into the street in front of them, his youthful curiosity getting the best of him. Marcus, who had been poking the empty cartridges out of the cylinder chambers and reloading them with fresh charges, saw the boy and on impulse tossed the empty cartridges to him. With a shout of delight, the boy scooped up the brass shell casings, just as the boy's mother called out to him, ordering him to stay away from "a man like that."

As they rode out of town, the boys pulled long, tan-colored coats, called dusters, from the back of their saddles, then put them on for the long ride. The dusters and the low-crowned, wide-brimmed hats created a type of uniform, and the way they automatically fell into a loose formation when they rode made them look like an army on the move. And that's exactly what they were.

Marcus Quinn, the leader, was tall, slim, blond, blue-eyed, and good looking. People said he could draw his Colt as quick as thought and shoot the eye out of a jack of spades from twenty paces. With a rifle, he could accomplish the same feat from sixty.

Hank Proudy, with his dark hair, dark, brooding eyes, and well-trimmed mustache, was stage-actor handsome. Though not particularly skilled with handguns, Hank was a smooth talker as well as a man of personal courage ... the kind of courage it took to get in close with a sawed-off Greener .10-gauge shotgun and shoot it out, toe to toe.

Billy Joe Higgins, six feet five, well over two hundred pounds, sporting long, red hair and a mountain man's beard to match, was the biggest of the group. Billy Joe carried a "Mare's Leg," a large-bore, short- barreled carbine that was sometimes called pocket artillery because of the hitting power of the projectile. The gun fit Billy Joe, because he was a man whose fists were almost as powerful.

Bob Depro's Choctaw Indian blood showed up in his dark hair, dark eyes, hairless chin, and prominent cheek bones. He was second only to Marcus in his skill with weapons; he was second only to Billy Joe in his strength. His weapon of choice was a bull whip. He was so skilled with the lash that he could flick a fly off the end of a man's nose without making the man flinch. The same lash could be used to take the skin off a man's back or break every bone in his body.

Loomis, Bob's younger brother, had the same dark, brooding features as Bob. He was not only the youngest of the group, he was also the smallest. Everyone tended to look out for Loomis, and sometimes he was resentful of it because he wanted to be his own man. Loomis's weapon of choice was the knife, and he could throw it or use it in a fight with equal skill. His quickness made him a dangerous adversary, no matter how large his opponent might be. Because of Loomis's weight and size, he was an outstanding rider who often supplemented the income of the group by entering and winning horse races.

Dislocated by the war and with no family or friends waiting for them back in Mississippi, Quinn's Raiders owed allegiance to no one except each other. As Marcus had just proven to the townspeople in Flagstaff they were individually more than anyone wanted to handle. Together . . . they were practically invincible.

The sheriff stood in the middle of the street and watched the five riders until they were gone, then he turned and walked back into his office, sat at his desk, and took out the two dodgers he had found on two of the three men who had just been killed.

The deputy sheriff came into the office then and

CHAPTER TWO

Hank expectorated loudly, then wiped the back of his hand across his mouth.

"I swear, I got that much dust in my mouth, General Pemberton coulda built breastworks around Vicksburg that Grant would still be tryin' to climb."

Billy Joe chuckled. "That happens to you ever'time you go more'n two days without a drink," he said. "Now me, I'm hungry."

"When you ain't hungry?" Marcus asked.

"Billy Joe, I got some beans soakin' in a bag," Loomis said. "We get camped, I'll cook 'em up good."

"One of these days, Loomis, you're gonna make a fella a good wife," his brother Bob teased, then ducked quickly to avoid Loomis's punch.

"I see a stream up ahead," Marcus said. "Might as well make camp before it gets dark."

Bob constructed a rope remuda, and the boys

dismounted, then dropped their saddles. Loomis built a fire and put the beans in a pot.

To the west the sun was dropping toward the foothills, while to the east evening purple, like bunches of violets, began gathering in the notches and draws of the red mountains. Behind the setting sun, great bands of color spread out along the horizon.

Marcus walked over to watch Loomis as he poured the presoaked beans into a pot of water he had scooped from the stream.

"Can't promise much for our supper," Loomis said. "We ain't got no bacon for flavorin'. Might have an onion or two left. Maybe a couple of peppers."

"We need to find us a town, Marcus," Bob said. "We runnin' out of ever'thing."

"Yep," Marcus said. "Only thing, they ain't no signs pointin' the way to tell us where the closest town is."

"Hell, I can take care of that," Hank said. He climbed up on a rock then made a great show of sniffing the wind. He turned all the way around, then stopped. He raised one foot, then leaned forward and pointed to the northeast.

"There!" he said. "I smell whiskey and women comin' from that direction."

The others laughed at his antics, and Billy Joe started to say something when they heard a sudden outbreak of gunfire. Hank jumped down from the rock.

Though it wasn't dark yet, Loomis, in what was

almost a reflex action, dumped the pot of beans onto the fire, smothering it out. By now all five men were on their bellies, guns in hand. From long experience, they had automatically formed themselves into a defensive ring with each man taking one-fifth of the circle around them, thus covering the entire area.

"Anyone see anything?" Marcus asked.

"Nothin' here," Hank answered, and his response was repeated all the way around the circle.

They heard another outbreak of gunfire, and this time they could tell the direction from which it was coming. They could also tell that the gunshots weren't directed toward them.

"Shit," Loomis said, standing up and holstering his pistol. "Looks like we lost our supper for nothin'."

"What you reckon it is?" Billy Joe asked.

"Don't know," Marcus answered. "What say we get saddled and go find out?"

As Marcus and the others rode toward the sound of battle, they found themselves being funneled down a small, narrow pass. The gunshots rolled up toward them, bouncing from wall to wall and filling the pass with an avalanche of sound. When they reached the other end of the pass, they saw that it opened onto a small valley. At the edge of the valley, a wooden shack nestled beneath an overhang in the shadows of a cliff. They wouldn't have seen the shack at all, had a muzzle flash from the window not called their attention to it.

From the boys' position at the mouth of the pass,

the cabin was about fifty yards to their right, while the rocky ledge, toward which the shooter in the cabin was firing, was about twenty-five yards to the boys' left. The shot from the cabin hit the rocky ledge and ricocheted off with a high-pitched whine which reverberated through the canyon.

Marcus and the others were safe where they were, but they could go no further without getting caught in the crossfire.

"There," Loomis said. "I see the others."

The men attacking the house were huddled in a group behind the rocky ledge. There were at least ten of them, though only one or two were actually firing at the house. The others were standing around, smoking and passing a bottle of whiskey back and forth. Marcus saw, also, that they had a prisoner, a man who was bound and gagged, sitting on the ground, leaning against one of the rocks.

"They're all wearin' badges," Bob noted, and Marcus saw them also. A couple of the badges were shining bright red in the light of the setting sun.

"What are we gonna do, Marcus?" Loomis asked.

"We ain't gonna do nothin'," Marcus said. "This ain't our fight."

There was another exchange of gunfire between the posse and the shack, and Marcus and his men could hear the bullets plunking through the front wall of the cabin.

One of the men in the posse drained the rest of the

whiskey from the bottle, then threw it against the rocks. The man wiped his mouth with the back of his hand and scratched his crotch. He crawled up to the ledge and stood behind the two who were shooting toward the house.

"Hey, you squaw!" he yelled. "Come on outta that goddamned shack, or we're gonna come get you!"

There was no answer from the house.

"Hey, Pete, you gonna talk her to death?" someone asked, and the others laughed.

"Well, come on, we gonna kill that Injun bitch or ain't we?" Pete asked, looking at the two men who were pointing rifles toward the house.

"What do you want from us? Take an army to get her outta there."

"Goddamnit, we got an army. They's ten of us, only one of her. And we got the law on our side."

A new man came up, one the boys hadn't noticed before. Even from here, they could see how white he was, his skin, his hair.

"Look at that fella," Loomis whispered. "You ever seen a man *that* white?"

"Looks a little like a maggot, don't he?" Bob observed.

"If you don't like the way I'm runnin' things, you go get her," the maggot said.

"Fenton, you know I don't mean nothin' 'bout you, it's just..."

"I said go get her," Fenton said.

Pete held the rifle for a second, then he got a determined look on his face. "All right, by God, I will," he said.

Pete took two steps toward the house. There was a flash and the bark of a rifle, then he spun around with a hole pumping blood from his chest.

Marcus watched as the man stumbled, then fell to the ground.

"She shot Pete!" one of the others yelled, and all the rest came to the top of the ledge and began firing into the shack. They fired a heavy fusillade for several seconds, then a white flag fluttered pathetically from the window.

"Stop shooting!" Fenton said to the others. "Let's see what she's got to say."

"Is my man alive?" an Indian woman's voice called from the shack.

"Yeah, he's alive."

"I want to see him."

"Get McCabe up here," Fenton ordered, and two men jerked the prisoner to his feet and pushed him roughly up to the top of the rocks.

"I want to talk to him!"

"Sure, you can talk to him," Fenton said. "We'll let you talk to him just before we hang him. Now get your ass on out here."

"I want to talk to him now."

"All right. Come on out, we'll let you talk to him," Fenton said. "Get his gag off," he said more quietly.

The door opened, and a lone figure stepped onto the porch cautiously, hesitantly. Marcus saw a short, dumpy-looking Indian woman. She was carrying a rifle, but she leaned the rifle against the front wall of the shack.

"When she gets away from the rifle, shoot her," Fenton said.

"Sasha! Go back inside! It's a . . ." That was as far as McCabe got with his warning before someone brought a pistol butt down sharply on his head. He went down.

Back at the cabin, Sasha, who had heard her man's warning, started back toward the door. But she didn't make it. A rifle barked, and the Indian woman fell against the front wall, then down to the porch. She tried to get up, but the rifle barked a second time, and this time she fell back on the porch, her arms spread to either side of her.

"You got her, Fenton!" someone shouted excitedly.

Bob raised his pistol and took aim at the man they now knew as Fenton, but Marcus put his hand up gently and pulled it down.

"Did you see what that maggot-lookin' bastard did?" Bob hissed. Bob was part Indian, and he was boiling over with rage at what he had just seen.

"Bob, killin' that sonofabitch don't mean spit to that squaw now," Marcus said. "And we got no need to get involved in a fight that ain't ours."

"Marcus is right, Bob," Hank said.

"If it had been a white woman, would you feel the same way?" Bob asked.

"Bob," Loomis said to his brother sharply. "You got no call to say that to Marcus. Me an' you ain't never had no better friends than these men."

Bob ran his hand through his coal-black hair, then he sighed.

"Sorry, Marcus. I was just pissed off, that's all."

"Hell, Bob, you never been the cool-headed sort," Marcus said. He put his hand on Bob's shoulder and squeezed it.

"They ain't a one of us don't feel like you do," Billy Joe said. "But you know Marcus is right. Why buy into somethin' that don't concern us?"

"I think they're leavin'," Hank said.

The boys watched as the posse swung onto the horses. McCabe, still bound and gagged, was put on a horse, and the men could see him looking back with pained eyes at the woman who lay dead on the porch of the small cabin.

"Let's go, McCabe," Fenton said. "Don't worry none 'bout your woman. You'll be joinin' her up in that happy huntin' ground soon enough."

The posse rode off with their prisoner without taking time to bury the woman they had just killed. None of them even bothered to look back.

Marcus waited until they were out of sight, then he went up to the cabin and looked down at the woman. She had a round, moonlike face, a dumpy figure, and a nose that was too large. She was not at all a pretty woman, but she had been a woman who gave her life for her man, and in Marcus's eyes, that made her as good a woman as any he had ever seen.

"We ought to bury her," he said.

"Let Loomis and me take care of her," Bob asked. "We'll find a place she'd like."

"All right," Marcus agreed. He looked around the little cabin, noticing the bullet holes in the front wall and door. "I'll say this for her. She put up one hell of a fight."

By the time Bob and Loomis came back half an hour later, Billy Joe had cooked a stew from the stores he had found in the cabin. Quinn's Raiders were a practical bunch, having learned during the war to take advantage of every situation that presented itself. Though all of them felt some sympathy for the Indian woman who had been killed defending this shack, they felt no compunction about eating the food she left. Even Bob and Loomis ate with a hearty appetite.

"Marcus, if they was that many men in a posse, then that means there's got to be a town somewhere's close by," Hank observed.

"Yeah, the question is, do we want to go to a town that's got that much law?" Bob asked. "Ever' damn one of 'em was wearin' a badge. It was more like they was deputies than regular possemen."

"Yeah, I noticed that, too," Billy Joe said. "Who you reckon they was, Marcus?"

"I don't know," Marcus answered. "But we got no choice. We got to go into town and get some supplies." Hank smiled. "And have a few drinks."

Now it was Bob's time to smile. "And a town large enough to have that many deputies is bound to have a few friendly women around."

"You mean whores?" Loomis asked.

"Of course I mean whores, little brother. They're the friendliest of them all."

Marcus and his men spent the night in the cabin, then left the next morning, following the trail left by the posse. They figured by trailing the posse they'd find the town.

They had been riding for no more than an hour when Marcus held his hand up to stop them and stared off into the distance.

"What you lookin' at?" Hank asked.

"I was just wonderin' what's got their attention," Marcus said, pointing to the sky.

"Vultures," Loomis said.

"We've seen a few of them in the past," Hank said. Hank was right. Marcus Quinn and his Raiders had watched the vultures gather over battlefields from Texas to Tennessee, and from Alabama to Missouri. They had learned to recognize the differences in the ways the vultures behaved when they were circling over a human carcass and when they were over something else. These birds had definitely found a human carcass.

"Could be the men we saw last night was at work again," Bob said.

"Yeah," Billy Joe said. "They might of found 'em another woman to kill."

"You want to check it out?" Hank asked.

"Yeah," Marcus answered, loosening his pistol in his holster. Hank loaded his Greener, Billy Joe his Mare's Leg, and the men urged their horses into an easy, ground-eating gait.

The road sloped up gradually in front of them, cresting about one hundred yards away. Marcus pointed to it, and all five men were ready for anything when they came over the top. When they crested the hill, they saw the corpse of a man dangling from the long, straight branch of a big cottonwood tree. The corpse was twisting slowly at the end of the rope and even from here, the men could hear the creaking sound the rope was making.

"Marcus, you know who that is?" Loomis asked.

"Yeah, it's the fella the posse had last night."

"They lynched him," Loomis said. "Whatever he done, I figured they'd at least bring him back into' town for a trial."

"Shit," Bob said. "The least the bastards coulda done was cut him down."

"What kind of law is this up here?" Loomis asked.

"Loomis, can ya cut 'im down?" Billy Joe asked. "I don't like to see nobody just hangin' there like that, no matter what he done."

"Yeah, cut 'im down," Marcus said.

"You fellas remember the spy they hung back in Chattanooga that time?" Hank asked as the Raiders rode toward the hanging corpse.

"Yeah, I remember," Bob answered. "It was a Yankee lieutenant dressed up like a preacher. General Van Dorn caught 'im and strung 'im up."

"That was just before Dr. Peters found the general in bed with his wife and killed him," Marcus added.

"I know what you're gettin' at," Hank said. "You're tellin' me I ought to let that be a lesson to me." Hank was referring to the fact that he was very partial to married women and on more than one occasion had just barely managed to slip out the bedroom window as the woman's husband was coming through the front door.

"Unless you want to wind up shot," Marcus said. "From lookin' at this fella, I tell you one thing. I'd rather be shot than hung," Bob said.

When the five men reached the corpse, they saw a notice tacked to the boot of the victim. Marcus rode up to take a closer look. His horse wasn't spooked, but the animal was sensitive to the fact that the thing hanging from this tree was a dead man, and he didn't like it. The horse pawed at the ground nervously, and Marcus patted him reassuringly on the neck.

"What's the note say?" Billy Joe asked.

Marcus tore the notice off and read it aloud. "Notice to all land grabbers. This here is Luke McCabe.

He tried to get his land the easy way. His case was tried by the Commission. He'll stay here for others to learn about stealing. Chief Commissioner Fenton, town of Ristine."

"Tried by the Commission?" Hank asked. "What the hell commission're they talkin' about?"

"I don't know," Marcus answered. "But whatever it is, they're serious about it. Cut 'im down, Loomis." Loomis stood in his stirrups so he could reach the rope around McCabe's neck, then began sawing at the rope. With Loomis engaged and the others watching, they paid no attention to the riders who were coming down the road from the opposite direction.

"Hey, you! What do you think you're doin'?" one of them called angrily.

"Boy, get away from that body," the other man ordered.

Loomis looked at Marcus. "What you want me to do, Marcus?"

"Don't be askin' him," one of the two riders said. He pointed to the badges he and the other rider were wearing. "We're commissioners. We give the orders around here."

Loomis looked at the two men. Though they were blustering officially, neither of them had drawn a weapon.

"I don't know what the hell a commissioner is," Loomis said. "But the only one gives me orders is Marcus Quinn."

"Go ahead and cut 'im down," Marcus ordered.

"Mister, we're the law here," one of the two commissioners said. "You're goin' ag'in the law. Now, if you don't put that knife away . . ."

Hank cocked his sawed-off shotgun, and Billy Joe laid the barrel of his Mare's Leg across the saddle.

"Commissioners . . . law, don't neither one mean shit to us," Hank said. "Now, why don't you boys just ride on out of here while you can still do it sittin' up."

The two commissioners looked at each other in a moment of indecision, then with frustration on their faces, they turned to leave.

"When Quiet Charley Fenton finds out about this, he ain't gonna like it much," one of them said. They slapped their legs against their horses, then rode back in the direction from which they'd come.

Loomis cut through the rope, and McCabe's body fell to the road.

"What now?" Bob asked.

"We buried his woman," Marcus said. "We may as well bury him."

Two of the Raiders had small spades in their tack, so it didn't take long to open a shallow grave and lay the remains of the late Mr. McCabe inside. They buried him without ceremony or words, though Billy Joe did take off his hat.

"All right," Marcus said. "Let's see what this town of Ristine has to offer a thirsty man."

The town of Ristine had all the earmarks of a boom

town. False-fronted shanties and substantial two-story buildings were competing with canvas tents for space along both sides of the street. The street was noisy with the sound of hammering and sawing, while half a dozen wagons of commerce creaked up and down the street.

"Look there, Marcus," Hank said, pointing to a structure that was wooden sided but roofed with canvas at the end of the street. A large sign erected alongside the structure read: KANSAS AND PACIFIC LAND MANAGEMENT COMMISSION, BARLOW GOODWIN, PRESIDENT. CHOICE PROPERTY ALONG K&P RIGHT-OF-WAY FOR SALE HERE.

"Well, that explains all the activity in this little town," Marcus said. "The Kansas and Pacific Railroad is coming through here."

"Yeah," Hank said. "I heard that's how the railroads raise their money. The government gives the railroad land along the right of way for building the railroad, and the railroad sells the land to pay for it."

"They sure ain't wastin' none of their money on a office building," Bob said, pointing to the canvas roof. "You'd think they'd want to put on a little better show than that."

"Maybe the town just wanted to build the more important buildin's first," Hank said, pointing to a saloon. It was one of the more substantial buildings in Ristine, and the men rode toward it, then dismounted and went inside.

Though it was still midafternoon, the saloon was already crowded and noisy with the sounds of idle men and painted women having fun. Near the piano three men and a couple of the women filled the air with their idea of a song, the lyrics a bit more ribald than the composer intended.

"Yes, sir, what can I do for you gentlemen?" the bartender asked, sliding down toward them. He was wearing a stained apron and carrying a towel he used to alternately wipe off the bar then wipe out the glasses.

"What's your whiskey?" Hank asked.

"Got some Old Overholt. Two dollars the bottle, ten cents the drink."

"Leave the bottle," Marcus said, slapping the necessary silver on the counter.

The bartender put the bottle and five glasses on the bar, and Hank began to pour.

"Marcus, looks like we're gonna have some company," Loomis said under his breath.

Marcus looked into the mirror behind the bar and saw that the nine men were coming toward them. Among the number were the same two who had accosted them on the road outside of town. Marcus turned to face them.

"Somethin' I can do for you gents?" He asked.

"We was wonderin' what you did with McCabe's body," one of the two he had met earlier stated.

Marcus noticed that all the men were wearing

badges. He raised his glass and took a drink, then put the glass back on the bar.

"We buried him," he said quietly.

"Mister, we gave you orders to leave that body where it was," the spokesman of the group said. "Now you had us outnumbered on the road, but that ain't the case now, so I figure it's time we learned you a lesson."

"Yeah," one of the others said. He counted the five Raiders, then his own group. "We got nine to your five. Near 'bout two to one, I'd say."

"This ain't fair, Marcus," Loomis said.

One of the commissioners smiled. "Well now, sonny, that's just the way life is sometimes."

"The way it looks," Loomis went on, ignoring the man's comment, "one of us is only gonna get one.

"All right, which two you want?" Marcus asked.

"Why don't I just take the two loudmouths?" Loomis said.

Loomis was referring to the two men who had accosted them earlier.

"Go ahead, they're yours," Marcus said easily.

One of the loudmouths turned to the others with a broad smile on his face. "Will you listen to this snot-nosed kid here. You'd think he . . . unngh!" That was as far as he got, because Loomis suddenly and unexpectedly sent a vicious kick between the man's legs, scoring a direct hit with the point of his boot. The commissioner grunted in pain, doubled over, then went down. Loomis's sudden move had caught the others by such surprise that they looked at their felled partner in shock. Moving quickly and taking advantage of their hesitation, Loomis picked up a nearby chair and brought it crashing down over the head of the other commissioner who had accosted them on the road. Within the space of a couple of seconds, two of the group were on the floor, one writhing in pain, the other out cold.

"All right, I got my two," Loomis said. "You boys can have the rest."

Marcus, Hank, Bob, and Billy Joe stepped away from the bar and faced the remaining seven commissioners. The commissioners had not noticed, until that moment, how big Billy Joe was, and as he stepped toward them, the whole line moved back.

"Tanner, go get Fenton," one of the men said nervously, and Tanner started out the door of the saloon. A couple of others dragged the two men Loomis had hit back with them to the far corner of the saloon. The patrons of the saloon, convinced now that the show was over, went back to their private conversations, and the place grew noisy again.

As the boys stood at the bar drinking their whiskey, Marcus saw Tanner come back into the saloon. With him was the man they had seen last night, the one the others called Fenton.

Examining him closely, Marcus saw that it hadn't been a mere trick of lighting last night. The man really was white. His skin was pale as chalk, his hair was white, and his eyes were pink. Tanner pointed to Marcus and the others, and Fenton studied them for a moment, then went over to join the other commissioners.

"Who's the guy that looks like a maggot with pink eyes?" Marcus asked the bartender.

Marcus saw a look of fear cross the bartender's face, and he looked nervously toward the albino.

"Mister, don't ever let him hear you talk like that," the bartender cautioned.

"He supposed to be dangerous, is he?" Hank asked.

"That's Charley Fenton," the bartender said. "They say he's killed more'n ten men already."

"And at least one woman," Bob snorted.

"What's that?" the bartender asked.

"I noticed on a sign comin' into town that he's the chief commissioner. What's that mean?" Marcus asked, ignoring the bartender's question.

"It means he's the law," the bartender said. "Excuse me, I got business to tend to." The bartender hurried down to the other end of the bar, as much, Marcus decided, to get away from the uncomfortable questions as to do any actual work.

A moment later another man came into the saloon, then smiling, walked toward the Raiders. He had his hand extended toward Marcus.

"Gentlemen, gentlemen, on behalf of the Kansas and Pacific Railroad, let me welcome you to Ristine. I'm Barlow Goodwin."

ROBERT VAUGHAN

Goodwin was of average size with dark hair, dark eyes, and a dark Vandyke beard. He was well dressed and prosperous looking.

"You the mayor of this town?" Hank asked.

"The mayor?" Barlow replied. He laughed. "Well, I guess you could almost say that. You see, Ristine hasn't been formally incorporated yet, so it doesn't actually have a governing body. That's why the Kansas and Pacific Land Management Commission has assumed some of the responsibilities of government. So naturally, as president of the commission, I am the man everyone turns to when they need help. Mr. Fenton, as my chief commissioner, functions rather like the chief of police, while members of the commission act as police officers."

"Yes, we've met a couple of them," Marcus said. He pointed toward the table where the two men Loomis had attacked were just now beginning to recover.

Barlow took out an expensive-looking cigar, bit the tip off, then lit it before he spoke again.

"I've come to apologive for any trouble my men may have caused you," he said.

"No need." Marcus said.

Barlow laughed. "No, I guess there isn't. You seem to have caused a little trouble for them."

"We don't want trouble," Marcus said.

"I guess my men were just a little disturbed that you cut down McCabe's body. You see, McCabe was an outlaw, and the commission thought that perhaps leaving him up as an example to others ...

"Why didn't you bring in his wife's body, too?" Bob asked.

"Beg your pardon?"

"His wife," Bob said. "Your commissioners shot her down last night."

"Yes, well, that was a tragic circumstance," Goodwin said. "I didn't learn about that until this morning. It seems she opened fire on them when they went to arrest McCabe. As I understand it, my men had no choice but to return fire, and in the fight, Mrs. McCabe was killed. That is, if she actually was Mrs. McCabe. Some say she was just. . ."

"That what some say?" Bob asked.

"Yes." Suddenly Goodwin looked more closely at Bob, as if seeing the Indian features for the first time. "Look here, this woman, did you . . . did you know her?"

"No."

"Oh. Well, like I said, it was tragic, but some things simply can't be avoided. None of this would have happened if McCabe had obeyed the law. He thought that because he had lived on a piece of land for over ten years, it was his. I showed him a government deed declaring that the land was the property of the Kansas and Pacific Railroad. I offered to sell it to him at the going rate, but he refused to do business with us. Then, when we found it necessary to clear him off the land, he fired on us, wounding one of my men. After that we went back, this time with enough force to get the job done. I can assure you, we do have the law on our side."

"I don't know much about the law," Marcus said. "And truth to tell, I never cared much for it or for the people who put on badges to enforce it. But I never thought lynchin' was legal."

"Oh, it wasn't a lynching," Barlow said. "He was tried before a board of commissioners and found guilty. Since there is no other law in effect here, that's about as legal as it's gonna get."

Marcus poured himself another drink, then studied Barlow for a moment over the rim of his glass.

"Look, Barlow," he finally said. "It don't make any difference to me whether it's legal or not. I didn't know McCabe, so I got no problems with it one way or the other. My pa always told me I was gonna wind up hung, so I don't like seein' someone trimmin' a tree. That's why we cut the man down. But, like I said, we're not lookin' for trouble. So if you and your commissioners want to play law, you go right ahead. Just keep them the hell out of our way, and we'll stay out of theirs."

"Good enough," Barlow agreed, smiling broadly. "Dutchman, give these boys another bottle of whiskey on me."

"Yes, sir, Mr. Barlow," the bartender answered. After Goodwin left, Bob took a drink, then looked up at the bartender. "Barkeep, your whiskey's good," he said, stroking his chin, "but I was wonderin' if maybe this town didn't have a few other things a man might need."

"I beg your pardon?"

"What my brother's talkin' about is a whorehouse," Loomis said.

The bartender smiled and shook his head.

"Gentlemen, you'll be pleased to learn that Ristine not only has a whorehouse, it has the finest whorehouse in all Nevada Territory. Fact is, it's also a fine hotel with good rooms and a bath."

"And where might this place be?" Bob asked.

"It's the last buildin' at the north end of town on the other side of the street. You can't miss it."

"What you say, Marcus?" Bob asked. "Can we check it out?"

"Yeah, Marcus, how about it?" Hank added. "I don't know about the rest of you, but I'd like to take a bath and get into some clean duds, then maybe come back down here and find a friendly game of cards." Marcus agreed. He put the cork back in the half-empty bottle of whiskey, then put it and the full bottle Goodwin just bought for them under his arm.

Though Goodwin left the saloon after his conversation with the boys, Fenton did not. He was still there, standing just inside the door, staring at the Raiders. When they left, his eyes followed them, and he moved up to the bat-wing doors to watch as they mounted their horses and rode down the street.

41

"How long we gonna stay in this town, Marcus?" Hank asked.

"Don't know," Marcus replied. "There's whiskey, food, place to sleep, and women. . . . I'm not in any hurry to ride right back out. Are you?"

"No," Hank said. "I was just wonderin' how long it'll be 'fore one of us has to kill that rabbit-eyed sonofabitch that's been watchin' us from the saloon, is all."

CHAPTER THREE

THE GRAND HOTEL WAS MADE OF WOOD, TWO STORIES high, with a second-story balcony that ran all the way around the building. Below the balcony at the street level was a fine wooden porch with a dozen rocking chairs. A drawn-up little man with wire-rim glasses and white hair got up from one of the chairs and moved slowly down the steps to take the reins of the horses.

"Greetin's, gents, my name's Clarence. Are you boys just visitin' the girls, or will you be takin' rooms?"

"Maybe both," Marcus said.

"If you're takin' rooms, I'll take your horses 'round to the stable." He looked at the horse Loomis was riding. "That's a fine-lookin' animal you got there, son," he said. "Looks like he can run some."

Loomis smiled. "Clarence, you're a pretty good judge of horseflesh," he said.

"We got us a horse race cornin' up soon," Clarence said. "Maybe you'll want to enter it."

"Maybe I will," Loomis said. "You take good care of the animals."

"Like'n they was my own," Clarence said. He started toward the back of the hotel leading the five mounts, lighter now by the saddlebags each man had removed.

"You boys just go on inside an' tell Elam, that's my brother, that you'll be stayin' here. He'll give you keys, get you sent up to your rooms, take good care of you." For such a small town, the lobby of the Grand Hotel seemed huge. There were a dozen or more chairs and sofas scattered about, several potted plants, mirrors on the walls, and a grand, elegant staircase rising to the second floor.

"What can I do for you gents?"

"You'd be Elam?" Marcus asked.

"Yes, sir."

"Elam, we need a place to stay."

"We got one large room that's nice, if you boys want to share."

"We'll take three rooms," Marcus said. "They'll share a room," he pointed to Bob and Loomis Depro, "and they'll share one." This time he pointed to Hank and Billy Joe. "I'll take one to myself."

"Very good, sir," Elam answered. He took the keys down from a row of nails and gave all three to Marcus. There was no registration ledger. "Rooms are fifty cents the night... in advance."

Marcus gave the man a dollar and a half, then passed out the keys.

"You got a place to take a bath in this hotel?" Hank asked, rubbing the stubble on his chin.

"Yes indeed, sir, the girls insist upon it," Elam answered. He smiled. "We even have a water tank on the roof so that we have running water."

While Elam was explaining how to get to the bathroom and use the running water, Bob was looking anxiously through the lobby. There was absolutely no one in sight except for the boys themselves and the clerk. Finally, Bob turned to the old man with a questioning expression on his face.

"Where the hell are they, Elam?"

"I beg your pardon, sir?"

"I thought this here was a whorehouse."

"Oh, it is, sir. One of the finest," Elam said proudly. "Well?"

"Well, what, sir?"

"Well, goddamnit, where the hell are the whores?"

"I suspect most of them are sleeping. They work nights, you know."

"Can you roust one of them up?"

"Yes, sir," Elam replied. "Which one?"

"Which one?" Bob asked, laughing. "Hell, man, I don't know none of 'em, so it don't make no difference. Just choose one. Choose the one you like best."

"Well, sir, they're all fine-lookin' ladies. I don't

reckon I have a favorite. But I believe I did see Suzie up a few moments ago. I'll send her to your room."

"Fine, fine," Bob said, rubbing his hands together in anticipation. He turned to Loomis. "Little brother, looks like you're gonna have to find some place to go. I'm gonna be usin' the room for a while."

"All right," Loomis agreed. "Me and Billy Joe'll take a look around anyway, see what they got in this town."

An hour later Hank had scrubbed and shaved, and Loomis and Billy Joe were exploring the town, while Bob was entertaining Suzie in his room. With the bathroom finally available, Marcus drew a fresh bath and settled into the large brass bathtub to scrub away the residue of the long ride. A clean shirt and clean pair of pants hung over the back of a nearby chair. On the floor beside him was half a glass of whiskey, and beside the glass, what was left of the first bottle of Old Overholt. The new bottle, the bottle Goodwin bought them, was back in his room, still untouched. A cigar was elevated at a jaunty angle from his freshly shaved face, and Marcus was trying to wash his back while at the same time singing, "The dew is on the grass, Lorena. . . ."

His singing was interrupted by the sudden and unexpected opening of the bathroom door. When he looked around, he saw a very pretty young woman step into the room. She was a strawberry blonde with green eyes, and dimples. The dimples showed deeply when she smiled, and she was smiling broadly.

"Uh . . . can I help you, miss?" Marcus asked.

"No, but maybe I can help you. If you'll stop that infernal racket, I'll wash your back for you." She picked up the wash cloth and dipped it in the water then started running it down his back.

"You telling me you don't care for my singing?"

"Is that what you call it? I've heard coyotes do better."

"Ahh," Marcus said in blissful appreciation. "A little more to the left, if you don't mind.

There, that's it! Of course I call it singing. Uh, listen, honey, if you're lookin' for a little business ..."

"I've already got your business," the woman said, interrupting him. "My name's Maggie Pettibone, and I own this place."

"I see. Do you provide this kind of service for all your customers?"

"No," Maggie answered. "But none of my other customers have ever stood up to the commissioners the way you and your friends did."

"I take it you don't like the commissioners."

"They're bullies, and they have everyone in town terrified of them."

"Except you."

"Wrong. I'm terrified of them, too." Maggie dipped the cloth in the water and continued to wash his back. "How's this?"

"Fine, but you could do a better job if you came in with me," Marcus suggested.

"Don't get the wrong idea, Mr. Quinn. I run this place, but I'm not on the line myself."

"You mean you retired?"

"No. I never was on the line in the first place. I was a schoolteacher in St. Louis when I got a letter from a woman named Kate Wilson, offering me a most generous stipend to come out here and tutor her and her girls. Kate and I became friends, and when Kate was accidentally shot and killed by a drunken customer a couple of months ago, I learned that she left me the business."

Marcus chuckled. "Ownin' a whorehouse must've seemed like a shockin' idea to a school marm."

"Quite the contrary, Mr. Quinn. Having been on the periphery of 'the life' for almost a year, I found that I have no trouble with what goes on here. Besides, all the girls who work here are my friends. If I closed the place down, I'd be turning them out into the street, now wouldn't I?"

"Miss Pettibone, are there any clean towels left?" a woman asked, coming into the bathroom then. She hadn't bothered to knock, and now she left the door standing wide open.

"I'll get them, Suzie," another girl said, appearing from the hall at that moment. "They're out back. I haven't taken them down from the line yet."

"Hi, Marcus," Hank said, stepping into the bathroom. "That was Suzie. Pretty, ain't she? Listen, I'm goin' to find me a card game, you want to come along?"

"Mr. Quinn will be busy," Maggie said. "He's having dinner with me."

Clarence who had greeted them downstairs, came next. "Ah, Miss Pettibone, Elam told me you was up here. We're out of oats for these gentlemen's horses. You want me to go down to the mercantile and get some more?"

"Hold it! Just a goddamned minute here!" Marcus suddenly shouted. Everyone looked at him, surprised by his sudden outburst. "Is there a sign outside this door saying this is a meeting room? Goddamnit, I'm taking a bath here!"

"Hell, we can see that, Marcus," Hank said, and everyone in the room laughed.

"Get the hell out of here and close the goddamn door behind you."

Hank, Clarence, Suzie, and the other girl who had come into the bathroom left. Only Maggie Pettibone stayed behind.

"Did you mean for me to leave also?" she asked.

"I don't know. Have you ever considered going into 'the life'?"

Maggie smiled. "Why, Mr. Quinn. I do believe you may be propositioning me."

"I might be."

"Don't get me wrong, Mr. Quinn. I'm not some fresh, young virgin. It's just that I like to choose the men I'm with. You can't do that on the line." She knelt down on the floor beside the brass tub and kissed him.

Her mouth opened and their tongues met. She put her hand down in the water, then moved it toward the hard shaft of his throbbing penis. That was when Marcus stood up. She looked at him with confusion on her face, surprised by his sudden move.

"I'll be damned if I do this in a bathtub," he said. "My room's just across the hall."

Marcus wrapped himself in a towel, then grabbed his shirt and pants. The moment they were in his room, Maggie met him with another kiss. This time, she pressed her body hard against his, then opened her mouth hungrily to seek out his tongue. Marcus's arms wound around her tightly, and he felt the heat of her body transferring itself to his. She pulled the towel to one side, then ground her pelvis against his huge, exposed erection.

"Get out of your clothes," Marcus demanded, and Maggie stepped back from him, then smiled as she removed her dress, garment by garment, until she stood before him as naked as he.

"You like what you see?" she asked, turning and posturing before him.

"Too damned much talk," Marcus said, pulling her to him. He felt her naked breasts mash against his bare chest as they kissed again, then he picked her up and deposited her unceremoniously on his bed. He climbed on top, and she threw her arms around his neck, writhing and squirming beneath him. She spread her legs to receive him, and when he entered her, he felt her buck with the sudden rush of pleasure.

"Yes," she said, matching her rhythms to his in eager counterpoint.

Maggie was soft and pliant beneath him, and her skin was soft and hot as if burning with a fever. Though she had made it very clear to him that she wasn't a working girl, it was obvious that she was a woman who knew and enjoyed her pleasure.

Finally, Marcus could hold back no longer and he burst inside her. Maggie felt it, and she cried out with the pleasure of it and clasped him tightly to her as if unwilling to let him go.

Sated at last, Marcus collapsed atop her, until his breathing returned to normal. He felt good. He let out a sigh and rolled off her, then lay beside, listening to the receding sound of her raspy breathing, touching her soft belly.

"Thank you, Mr. Quinn," Maggie whispered.

Marcus raised up on one elbow and looked down at her. The breasts, which were small and hard when she was standing, were now only gentle curves. Only the nipples, hard and erect, interrupted the smooth lines of her body. He reached down to touch one, and she shivered in pleasure.

"It's a shame," she said.

"What's a shame?"

"That you'll be leaving town so soon."

Marcus chuckled. "We just got into town. What makes you think we'll be leaving it so quick?"

"You've got the commissioners against you," Maggie said. "Nobody's ever been able to stand up to them."

"That don't mean nobody can," Marcus said.

Down the street from the hotel, G. B. Greer, owner-publisher of the *Ristine Gazette*, lifted the page from the platen and held it up, the fresh ink still glistening black on the page. There was something about a newly printed newspaper, something that stirred the blood and made him want to shout out in pride.

The newspaper in Ristine was the fifth G.B. Greer had published. With a sturdy hand press and a heavy-freight wagon, he had loaded up press, type, imposing stones, ink, and paper, then come west. He had done well in two previous towns, but they had been boom towns that went bust when the small amount of gold that had caused their birth, played out. Two other towns seemed indifferent to the existence of a newspaper, but here in Ristine, he was actually beginning to show a profit. If he could only live long enough to enjoy it.

The words he printed today were pretty powerful words, more powerful than anything he had printed since setting up shop in Ristine. It was an indictment against the commissioners, against the so-called trial by which they justified the hanging of Luke McCabe.

Greer had felt from the beginning that the idea of having commissioners instead of real law officers was just a means of giving absolute control to one man. That one man was Barlow Goodwin, and as long as Goodwin had his own private army, he would continue to control Ristine and the lives of everyone who chose to live here.

Greer would never have been so bold as to print what he really felt had he not heard of the five men who cut down McCabe's body and buried it, despite the warning of the commissioners. Those same men then faced them down in the saloon.

By their action, those men had shown the others that the commissioners could be stood up to. And now, through the power of the words in his editorial, G.B. Greer would do the same thing.

"They say the pen is mightier than the sword," he said to himself as he looked over his page. "I guess we're about to find out."

Greer printed another two hundred copies, then he carried them out with him, leaving them at the locations about town where merchants agreed to sell his papers for him. One of the places where Greer left a stack of newspapers was the end of the bar at the Silver Dollar Saloon. He left a stack of fifty papers, picked up four left over from the day before, took forty-six cents out of a bowl where people who picked up the paper left their money, then walked back outside to continue his rounds.

CHAPTER FOUR

THE OWNERS OF THE SILVER DOLLAR SALOON HAD GONE
to great lengths to make it the gaudiest building in
Ristine. A long, gilt-edged mirror was on the wall
behind, while on the bar were several large jars of
pickled eggs and sausages. Towels were tied to rings
every few feet on the customers' side to provide the
patrons with a means of wiping their hands. Above the
mirror was a big sign which read: ONLY HONEST
GAMBLING IN THIS ESTABLISHMENT. PLEASE
REPORT   ALL   CHEATERS   TO   THE
MANAGEMENT.

In addition to the sign, the walls of the saloon had
other decorations, including game heads and pictures.
One of the pictures was of a reclining nude woman. An
anonymous marksman had added his improvement to
the painting by putting three bullet holes through the
woman in appropriate places, though one shot was

slightly off-target so that it looked as if her left breast had two nipples. The main room of the saloon was very large with exposed rafters below the high-peaked ceiling. There were at least a dozen tables and two potbelly stoves. As it was summer, the stoves stood cold, though soot and discolored metal were indications of previous use.

Hank stood at the bar just long enough to drink one whiskey. He watched the newspaper man shuffle in, leave his papers, then shuffle out. A couple of men in the saloon walked over and bought papers, then returned to their tables to read them. Hank had no interest in the papers, so he turned his back to the little pile and studied the room for a possible poker game.

Three cowboys were playing for tobacco and matches at one table, while a couple of women were sitting in on one of the other games. Hank liked women, but he didn't like them in his poker games.

The Raiders only had enough money for about two days, so he'd have to raise some, right away. The most likely game seemed to be in progress at a table near the stove at the back of the room. Four men were playing, each with a rather significant stack of money before them.

Hank finished his drink, then walked over to the table. One of the four players was wearing a badge. He looked up as Hank approached.

"Do somethin' for you, mister?"

"Private game?"

"I guess not," the commissioner said. He studied Hank through narrowed eyes. "You one of that bunch just rode into town, ain't you? Cut down McCabe's body?"

"That's right."

"The way you men acted, I didn't figure you'd be wantin' to do no socializin'."

"Don't figure on this bein' a social event," Hank said, pulling up a chair. "Figured this to be a serious game for some serious money," Hank said.

"And you've got some serious money to lose?" Hank smiled easily. "Well, I don't plan on losing it."

"I guess we'll just have to see about that. Ante up half a dollar."

As one of the other players shuffled the deck, the commissioner lit a cigar, then, when it was lit, pulled it from his mouth and examined the end of it for a moment.

"Seems like you was carryin' a sawed-off shotgun when you was in here before. You don't have it with you now?"

"Nope."

"And you ain't wearin' no pistol that I can see right now, neither."

"Nope."

"Probably ain't none too smart for you to be walkin' aroun' this town without you bein' armed. 'Specially since you done made a few enemies."

"How 'bout you? You one of my enemies?" Hank asked easily.

"Them was my friends your pard' roughed up."

"I'll tell Loomis to be careful next time," Hank said. "But you'll have to forgive him, he's still just a boy, you know, an' sometimes he gets a mite excited."

"You do that. And take my advice, start packin' a gun."

"I figure with so many badges around," Hank said, indicating the badge of the commissioner, "if anything comes up, I'll just go to the law."

"Haw," the commissioner said. "I reckon that's right. Any trouble come up, I'll handle it."

"Gentlemen," the dealer said. "Here come the cards."

Hank lost four dollars on the first hand. He was playing the cautious, timid soul, folding with a hand that would have been good enough to win, had he stayed in.

The commissioner chuckled as he dragged in his winnings. "Mister, you didn't have much luck, did you?"

"Maybe it'll get better," Hank said.

Hank lost the second hand by playing as timidly as he had in the first. Again the commissioner won, and again he laughed.

By the fourth hand, Hank was down twenty dollars; but there was over thirty dollars in the pot, and he had drawn two cards to complete a spade flush. Cautiously, he slid out five dollars.

"Whoa, hold on there, mister, you sure you want to bet?" the commissioner teased.

"I think I'm sure," Hank said.

"Well, it's gonna take a little gumption. What you got left?"

"Five dollars," Hank said.

"I'm gonna raise you that five dollars."

"Haggert, leave the man some money," one of the other players said. That was the first time Hank had heard the man's name mentioned. "It ain't sportin' to take ever' cent."

"He can hang on to it," Haggert said. "All he's gotta do is fold, and let me take the pot."

Hank slid his last five dollars out, then drew it back and looked at his cards, then slid it out again.

"All right," he said, hesitantly. "I'll call."

"Let's see what you got," Haggert said. He was holding three aces. When he saw that Hank beat him with a flush, instead of being angry, he laughed. "You was holdin' a flush and all you did was call?"

"I couldn't be sure," Hank said, pulling the pot in. "You might've had a bigger flush. I like to be certain. Anyway, I'm a little ahead of when I sat down."

Haggert leaned back in his chair and stroked his chin. "You think that makes you a winner, do you? Because you're a few dollars ahead?"

The commissioner's vanity was piqued at the thought of having lost to such a cautious nellie. That was exactly what Hank was planning.

It was Hank's deal. "I feel lucky now," he said. "I feel like betting the limit. Everyone ante a dollar." "Oh, so now you're the big gambler, are you?" Haggert said. "If you're all that big, why don't we up the ante?"

"Up the ante?"

"To five dollars. You got the guts?"

"All right," Hank said, pretending to be manipulated by the commissioner.

Hank took the deck and felt the cards as he began shuffling, checking for pinpricks and uneven comers. When he found none, he knew they were playing with an honest deck. He dealt. The betting was brisk, and within a few moments, the pot was well over two hundred dollars.

"Now, Mr. Gambler," Haggert said, "it's time we got down to it." He slid twenty dollars toward the center of the table.

"I'll see your twenty and raise you twenty," Hank said.

Haggert was a little surprised by Hank's reaction, but he saw Hank's twenty, and raised him fifty. "You want to see what I got, it's going to cost you."

The game had been for a few dollars at a time. Now, all of a sudden, there were a couple hundred dollars in the pot, and the betting was high enough to run the other three players completely out of the game. The stakes had also grown high enough to attract the attention of a dozen or more other patrons of the saloon, and they drifted over to stand by the table and watch the game unfold.

Hank smiled. Haggert had taken this game as a personal confrontation between the two of them, and that was just what he wanted.

"What about it, mister big gambler?" the commissioner asked. "It's just you and me now. You want to pay to see what I got?"

Hank's fish had bitten, now all he had to do was set the hook. He put his cards face down on the table and leaned forward, then smiled. With that move, his entire demeanor changed, and he was no longer the sputtering, hesitant, would-be gambler. He was cold and smooth.

"That's not the question, Mr. Haggert," Hank said. "The question is, do you want to pay to see what I have?" He reached into his inside vest pocket where he was carrying the gang's poke . . . enough to back him for another three hundred dollars, if need be. This was money that was never used for day-to-day living expenses, but anyone who had a sure hand in cards could tap it anytime he needed. Hank knew he had a sure hand. "It's going to cost you one hundred and fifty dollars to take a look."

Haggert's mouth opened, and he looked at Hank in surprise. "What? What the hell kind'a cards have you got?"

"Sonofabitch!" one of the players who had dropped

out said. "Look at the way he put 'em down. Hell, Haggert, I bet he's got four of a kind."

"You got'ny idea how much money's in that pot?" one of the others asked.

Whispered questions were passed back and forth.

"You're bluffin'," Haggert said through a cloud of blue cigar smoke.

"I might be," Hank said easily.

"Bluffin'? This fella? Are you kiddin'? Don't you remember how he bet a flush? Hell, he's got four of a kind, I tell you."

The smile never left Hank's face.

"Well, what are you gonna do, Haggert? You gonna call, or what?" one of the bystanders asked.

"All right, goddamnit! The pot's yours," Haggert said, angrily throwing his own hand down. He had a full house, aces over tens.

"Thank you," Hank said, reaching for the pot.

"Wait a minute! What have you got?" Haggert asked.

Hank's cards were still face down on the table just as he left them, four in one pile, one in the other. He made no move to turn them over.

"I said, what have you got?" Haggert asked again.

"Haggert, you didn't pay nothin' to see them," one of the men around the table said. "He don't have to show you iffen he don't want."

"Goddamnit! Show 'em!"

"If you want to see them that bad, take a look," Hank invited.

Haggert turned up the cards. Instead of four of a kind, there was a pair of fours and a pair of sixes.

"What?" Haggert sputtered. "That's what you were betting? Two lousy pair?"

"I guess I just don't know how to play the game," Hank joked as he raked the money in.

Everyone laughed but Haggert. He failed to see the humor in it.

"You sonofabitch, I'm gonna kill you!" he shouted, reaching for his gun.

There was a clatter of overturned chairs and a scrape of tables as everyone pushed back away in quick fear to avoid catching an errant bullet. Though scrambling for their lives, they managed to keep their eyes open so as not to miss any of the drama. Hank got ready, watching as Haggert clawed for his pistol. He'd wait until the gun had cleared leather before he had his move. If he shot a commissioner without eyewitnesses seeing that it was a matter of self-defense, there might be a necktie party in his future.

At the last minute, just as the commissioner was raising the barrel of his Remington .31 and thumbing back on the hammer, Hank's right hand was suddenly filled with a four-barreled pepperbox, the small palm gun he kept up his sleeve when he played cards, and he fired. Though not accurate over a space of more than ten feet, at close range the weapon was deadly. He was less than that distance from Haggert now.

The commissioner, his eyes showing shock and

surprise, felt four .22-caliber bullets tear into his chest. His gun slipped from his hand, unfired, and he lurched back against the stove, knocking the pipe loose and scattering soot and charcoal onto the floor. He fell belly up, his chest soaked red with blood, his eyes open and unseeing.

"What the hell? Where'd that gun come from?" someone asked.

"It was a belly gun," another said.

Two more badge-wearing commissioners stepped forward, both of them holding pistols.

"Mister, that was our friend you just murdered."

"It weren't murder, it was self-defense, we all seen it," one of the other witnesses said.

"Yeah, you ain't gonna make murder stick."

"All right, we won't do it legal, we'll just do it," one of the two guntoters said.

"Yeah," the other added with an evil smile. "We'll just settle accounts here and now. You got 'ny more tricks up your sleeve, reckon you better use 'em now."

As Hank had discharged every barrel of his belly gun, he was completely defenseless. He took a step back, his eyes riveted on the two pistols pointed at him.

Suddenly, there was a loud cracking sound like the sudden peal of thunder close on behind a bolt of lightning. And like a bolt of lightning, a bolt of rawhide snapped out, whipped the guns from the hands of the two commissioners, then snapped back.

Both men cursed, grabbed their hands, and let out a

sharp bark of pain. Another commissioner in the crowd made the mistake of starting for his own gun, but the rawhide lash reached out and snapped his gun away as well.

Hank smiled and turned to see Bob standing just inside the doorway, holding his handmade rawhide whip.

"Get that sonofabitch!" one of the commissioners shouted, and again the whip snapped out, poppled like the peal of doom, then flipped back.

Everyone in the saloon backed away except the commissioners. With their pistols on the floor, there was very little they could do. Every time one of them made a try to pick up his gun, Bob would snap the whip again.,

"If I was you, boys," Hank said, "I'd stand perfectly still. Else you're liable to get in the way of the tip of that whip. And believe me, I've seen it take off skin." Another commissioner came into the saloon then, but before he could even reach for his pistol, Bob had snatched it from his holster with another adroit flip of the whip.

Finally, with all of them standing motionless and unarmed, Hank growled at Bob. "Get 'em out of here, Bob. They're smellin' up the place."

Bob smiled, then went to work, using the whip to cut strips out of the shirts and trousers of the commissioners, though holding back so that he was doing little more than stinging them. Cursing and yelling, the man hurried out the door with the laughter of the saloon's patrons chasing them into the street.

"Mister," one of the patrons said to Bob after the commissioners were gone, "I hope you're a drinkin' man, 'cause I aim to buy you one for givin' them men the comeuppance they deserve."

Bob folded up the whip then, and with Hank, stepped up to the bar.

"Well, I have been known to drink a few," he said with a big smile.

CHAPTER FIVE

ABOUT TEN MILES FROM TOWN, AT THE RANCH OF A MAN named Miner Cobb, Goodwin swung down from his horse. Charley Fenton, who had ridden out to the Cobb ranch with Goodwin, remained mounted, holding the reins to Goodwin's horse as Goodwin started up the path toward the house.

The house was small and unpainted, but the front yard was ablaze with summer flowers carefully planted and tended by Mrs. Cobb. On the side of the house, a garden of lettuce, tomatoes, beans, corn, and potatoes flourished.

"That's far enough, Goodwin," a man's voice said, and Miner Cobb stepped through the front door, carrying a long Civil War rifle in his hands. Behind him, peering tentatively out the door, was his wife, a handsome woman in her late thirties. Behind her still, a girl of about sixteen. There was a boy, too, Goodwin knew, a strapping fourteen-year-old, but he didn't see him.

Goodwin stopped when Cobb called to him.

"Mr. Cobb, no need of you actin' like that," he said. "1 come out here to make you a business proposition."

"I know what your proposition is," Cobb said. "And I ain't interested in takin' it. This here's my land, and I aim to hang on to it."

Goodwin sighed, took off his hat, and mopped his sweating forehead.

"It's hot, Mr. Cobb. Too hot to be standin' out here in the sun talkin' about this. Couldn't we discuss it inside."

"No."

"Miner, we don't need to be rude," his wife said. "Let him come inside."

"No need," Cobb said. "He ain't gonna be here long enough. Goodwin, I done told you, I ain't gonna sell my place. Now you and that fella that's with you get on back into town. 1 see you out here again, I don't plan on bein' so friendly."

Goodwin smiled, tried a joke. "Why, Mr. Cobb. You call this bein' friendly?"

"I didn't shoot you on sight, Goodwin. That's friendly enough," Cobb said.

Goodwin sighed, then started back toward his horse. He climbed on, then took the reins from Fenton.

"Mr. Cobb, I wish you had been more cooperative than this. The railroad can get a writ to force you to turn this land over to me. My offer won't be so generous next time."

"It don't matter whether your offer's for more or less," Cobb said. "The answer's gonna be the same ever' time."

"Come on, Mr. Fenton, we'll have to take other steps."

As the two men rode away, Cobb's wife saw the albino's eyes stare at her, and she shivered. It was as if she saw the fires of hell burning there.

"Who were those men, Mama?" her daughter asked. "You wouldn't even let me see them."

"I didn't want you to see them," the woman answered. "One of them, the white one with the pink eyes, has been touched by Satan. If an unmarried girl looks at him, her milk will turn sour at the first baby."

The young girl shivered, and Cobb reached out to put his arms around his two women.

"Hush now, woman. I won't be hearin' such nonsense," he said. "Just put the fear of that man out of your head. I've made it plain I ain't gonna sell this land; they won't be comin' out here no more."

That night Charley Fenton stood at the front door of the Kansas and Pacific Land Management Commission office, staring out at the town. Subdued winks of soft light shined from the windows of the houses back in the residential area of the town, while on Main Street half a dozen saloons spilled golden splashes of brightness onto the boardwalks. The street was noisy with piano playing, singing, drinking, and loud, raucous conversation. There was a man's hoarse guffaw and a woman's high-pitched cackle. Someone broke a glass somewhere, and the crashing, tinkling sound was supreme for a moment.

Then there came the sound of hollow hoof beats upon the street as a handful of drovers rode into town, passing in and out of light and shadow.

"Sounds like a live town," a voice said from a dark spot.

"Yeah, I'm gonna get somethin' to eat besides trail grub."

"Eat? I ain't gonna have time to eat.... I'm gonna get so drunk I don't even know where I'm at."

"Hell, Johnny, most of the time you don't know where you're at anyhow."

All the drovers laughed, then rode on beyond Quiet Charley's earshot. Behind him inside the office, a meeting was taking place. He turned back to it, then sat coldly, quietly, watching with expressionless pink eyes as one of the commissioners spoke his concern to Barlow Goodwin.

"We've got to do something, Mr. Goodwin. What if the rest of the town starts actin' like these fellas?" the commissioner asked.

"Yeah. We'd lose control," another added.

"The newspaper's already sayin' as how the folks should incorporate this into a real town, vote in a sheriff and city council and the like."

"You ask me, somebody needs to teach Greer a lesson."

Several others began expressing their own ideas at the same time, and Goodwin had to rap on the table in order to bring the meeting to order. Counting Goodwin and Fenton, there were eleven men at the meeting. Their number had been reduced by one ... the man Hank had killed earlier. Three of those present were wearing the marks of Bob's bullwhip. When Goodwin and Fenton returned from Cobb's ranch, he heard what happened and called an emergency meeting. He had not expected to be turned down by Cobb. He had not expected to read an editorial as defiant as the one the paper printed today. And he had not expected to have one of his men killed.

"All right, all right, calm down," Goodwin said. He put the hammer down on the table and leaned back in his chair to look out over the men gathered before him. Though it had a canvas roof, the building in which the meeting was taking place had a wooden floor and walls. Behind him a wall map showed the progress of the Kansas and Pacific Railroad. "End of Track" was just under twenty miles away, and a dotted line on the map indicated that the railroad would continue on, right through Ristine.

"What are we gonna do, Mr. Goodwin?"

"Look at you," Goodwin said disgustedly. "What a sorry bunch I picked when I picked you men."

The commissioners hung their head in shame at his admonishment.

"What were you when I found you? I'll tell you what you were. You were out-of-work drovers, ex-soldiers, drifters. None of you had a pot to piss in or any prospects of getting one until I put a badge on you. I not only gave you a job, I promised you a future." He pointed to the map on the wall behind him. "I told you men I would give each of you a prime piece of land next to the railroad, and I have done that, haven't I?"

"Yes," the men mumbled.

"Ristine is a company town, and the company is responsible for the law." Goodwin pointed to himself. "I am the company, gentlemen, so that means I am the law. I intend to keep it this way. ... I don't intend to let some ink-stained newspaperman whip up the town into changin' things. Now, if you men can't make the townspeople respect that law .. . you damn sure better make 'em fear it. And don't let a bunch of strangers send you runnin' with your tail tucked between your legs."

"Mr. Goodwin, you don't know what kind of men these here fellas are," one of the men who had felt the sting of Bob's lash said.

"All right, then, you tell me. What kind of men are they?"

"Well, sir, for one thing, they don't scare. . . . They don't scare none at all."

"Then, gentlemen," Goodwin said quietly, "if we

can't scare these men, I suggest you find a few people who do scare and show the town of Ristine that my law will be enforced."

"Yes, sir," one of them mumbled.

"Now get out of here and get to work. Patrol the saloons and streets, make your presence known." After the others left, Fenton came back over to sit down by the map.

"What about Cobb?" he hissed. "You gonna let him get away with what he done today?"

"No," Goodwin said.

"You want me to go back out there tonight?" Goodwin stroked his chin as he contemplated the question for a moment. "No," he finally said. "Not yet. First things first. Right now we got to make sure we don't lose control of this town."

At that same time at the far end of the street in the dining room of the Grand Hotel, Marcus and Maggie had just finished dinner. Loomis and Billy Joe came in, and Marcus invited them to join Maggie and him at the table.

"Boys, this is Maggie Pettibone. She owns the place."

"Pleased, ma'am," the boys said, slightly doffing their hats.

"My, what gentlemen."

"Nothin' more'n a little southern manners, ma'am," Billy Joe said.

"You are from the South, then?"

"We fought for Mississippi durin' the war. Marcus there, he was our cap'n."

"Course, the war bein' over an' all, we got no hard feelin's toward Yankees," Billy Joe said. "I always figured we was southerners 'cause that's where we was borned. Iffen we'd come from Ohio, we would'a fought for the North hard as we fought for the South."

"The war's over," Marcus said. "No use talking about it."

"Would you two men like something to eat?" Maggie asked.

"No, thank you, ma'am" Loomis answered. "Me'n Billy Joe just got up from the supper table. We found us a cafe down the street a ways."

"Ruby's?"

"Yes'm, I believe that was the name of it."

"It is a nice cafe," Maggie agreed, "and Ruby's a good cook. But I think our Helga is better. Don't just take my word for it, though. Eat here tomorrow, and you can decide for yourself."

"Well, maybe I'll try a little somethin' tonight," Billy Joe suggested. When Maggie signaled to the kitchen, Helga came to take Billy Joe's order. Helga was a tall, strapping woman in her late twenties. Her blond hair was tied back in a bun, but an errant strand had fallen across her bright blue eyes, and when she pushed it back, she left a smudge of flour on her cheek. Her eyes shone brightly as she looked at Billy Joe.

"You want something to eat, ya?" she asked in a thick Swedish accent.

"Uh . . . yeah," Billy Joe answered. He had been staring at her so intently that he had to bring himself back to give her his order. "Some biscuits, fried 'taters, maybe a mess of fried onions, a couple of steaks . . . you got 'ny pie?"

"Pie, ya, cherry and apple is what we have."

"I'll have a slice of each," Billy Joe ordered.

Helga smiled. "Is good to see a man that eats a good supper," she said.

"Supper?" Loomis chuckled. "Ma'am, he done et supper. This here is just a bite in between meals."

When Helga left the dining room, Maggie saw that Billy Joe's eyes followed her all the way to the kitchen. "She's pretty, isn't she?" Maggie asked.

"Oh, yes, ma'am," Billy Joe said. "She's 'bout the prettiest thing I seen in a long time."

"She came to America as a mail-order bride," Maggie explained. "She came over from Sweden to marry some little weasel of a storekeeper. When she got off the stage and he saw how much bigger than him she was, he packed up an' left town."

"You mean he run out on her?" Billy Joe asked as if unable to believe the story.

"That's what happened. Poor Helga, she'd used every cent she had in the world just to get over here. Then when he left town, she was broke with no place to go. Kate gave her a job ... told her she could work in the kitchen or go on the line...."

"So she took the kitchen," Marcus added.

"Yes," Maggie said. She got a pensive look on her face for a moment. "Truth is, I think she took the kitchen because she was feeling so low about her man running off that she was afraid no one would want her."

"Sure don't know why a woman as pretty as her would feel that way," Billy Joe said.

Later, as Billy Joe was concentrating on eating his meal, Marcus asked Maggie to tell him about Barlow Goodwin and the commissioners.

"He came a little over a year ago," Maggie said. "Until he came, Ristine wasn't much more than a stage-coach way station. Then Barlow Goodwin arrived with government deeds saying he owned all the land around Ristine, even land that was being ranched. With the deeds on his side, he used his commissioners to run everyone off, except McCabe, and you saw what happened to him."

"What's he been doing with the land?" Marcus asked.

"He's been selling to investors. He has a map showing the route of the railroad. He's made a fortune for the Land Commission, and Ristine has turned into a booming town. I've bought quite a bit of land myself."

"You?"

"Yes. I'm going to build a hotel."

"What do you mean?" Marcus asked, taking in the room with a wave of his hand. "You have a hotel."

"No, Marcus, I have a whorehouse," Maggie answered good-naturedly. "When the railroad comes through here, there'll be lots of visitors from the East. They'll be quality folks, and they'll want a place to stay, a real hotel."

"Tell us a little about these here commissioners," Loomis asked. "Are they really the law?"

The smile left Maggie's face. "Riffraff, the lot of them," she said. "At first the townspeople, the ones who were already in the area and the new ones who came in, thought it might be a good thing to have them to keep out the outlaws. But the way it's turned out they are much worse than any outlaw they might keep out."

"What about Fenton?" Marcus asked.

"Stay away from him," Maggie said with a shiver.

"Is he that fast?" Loomis asked.

"Fast? I don't know. You only know that about men who have been in gunfights. Quiet Charley Fenton doesn't have fights, he just kills people. He can shoot a man in the back as easily as he can step on a bug. As near as I can tell, he has no sense of human feeling whatever ... no hate, no love, no fear, no interest in women, no interest in whiskey, nothing. Killing is as easy for him as sneezing."

Marcus took a swallow from his coffee and thought about Maggie's words. Fast gunfighters, men who sold their speed, were, even the worst of them, a predictable breed. They had, at least, the common denominator of pride to drive them. Sometimes an opponent could use that pride to his advantage. Cold-blooded killers like Fenton, who had nothing in common with other men, were the most dangerous. Maggie need not have cautioned him to stay away from Fenton. Marcus intended to do just that.

There were about two dozen people in the Royal Flush saloon. At one table were the five young trail hands who had ridden into town earlier. They were going back south after a drive, but now they were playing cards and getting drunk on cheap whiskey. A cloud of noxious smoke from the strong "roll-your-owns" they were smoking hovered over the table. They had been exceptionally loud ever since they arrived, laughing uproariously at each other's jokes and comments.

"I heard tell they was gonna be a horse race here next Saturday," one of the cowboys said. "What say we hang around 'til then?"

"What for?"

"Well, hell, I'll ride in it, maybe win us a little money. You know I'm a good rider."

"You a good rider, Mills, but what you gonna ride? Them slab-sided critters we're ridin' now just got enough left in 'em to get us back down to Arizona."

"I sure hate to pass up the opportunity," Mills said.

"I tell you what I hate to pass up," one of the others said. "I hate passin' up the opportunity of visitin' the whorehouse in this town. Folks say it's one of the best."

"Well, I tell ya', Jed, that's just like me ridin' in the race," Mills said. "I ain't got no horse for the race," Mills said. "I ain't got no horse for the race, an' you ain't got enough money for the whores."

"No, but they's enough money in this pot for whoever wins to go down to the whorehouse," Jed said.

"Jed's right," one of the others said. "Come on, let's finish this hand."

"You think it's gonna be you that wins?" Jed asked. "Well, if it ain't me that wins, whoever does win is got to tell the rest of us all about it."

"What you got?"

"Two pair, aces and eights."

"Well, I got me a little full house, nines and sevens," Jed said. Amidst groans and grumbles, the other players showed their hands. Jed's little full house won.

Jed let out a happy whoop, then got up and started doing a little dance. His spurs tangled up, and he fell flat on his back.

"Hey, Jed, iffen your back's too bad hurt, I'll go down to the whorehouse for you," one of the others said amidst the laughter.

"Hell no, we'll send Johnny," Mills said, pointing to the youngest of their number. Johnny was so drunk, he'd passed out.

"The hell you say," Jed shouted. He hopped up. "You think I'm hurt? Give me your hat, I'm gonna do me a

Mexican hat dance." He grabbed a hat, then started dancing around it. But, as before, he got his spurs tangled and tripped, only this time instead of falling to the floor, he fell against another table. There were four men at that table, all four of them wearing the badges of commissioners.

"Get away from me, you drunken bastard!" one of the commissioners shouted, pushing Jed away.

"Mister, you don't have to get so mad about it," Jed replied.

"You're drunk and disturbin' the peace, all of you. Come on, you're goin' to jail."

The laughter stopped.

"No, sir, we ain't goin' to jail," Jed said. "Frank, go over there'n pick up Johnny. We'll just leave this town."

The four commissioners stood up.

"You're goin' to jail."

"No, sir, I done tole' you, we ain' goin' to no goddamn jail. We'll leave town, but we ain't goin' to jail. Come on, boys, we'll just back on out of here."

Jed and his friends started toward the door when the four commissioners suddenly drew on them.

"No, mister! Don't do that!" Jed shouted, and the cowboys had no choice but to draw their own guns. Both sides opened fire, and for a moment the room was alive with the flash and crash of gunfire. When the cloud of gunsmoke drifted away, one of the cowboys was lying dead on the floor along with two of the commissioners. The remaining commissioners were gone, having fled though the back door.

"Oh, Jesus," Jed said. "Mills. Mills, are you dead? Look at him, Frank."

"He's dead," Frank said. "Wes is hurt."

"How bad?" Jed asked.

"Jesus," Wes said, his voice strained with pain as he sat down heavily in a nearby chair. Blood was oozing though the fingers of the hand he was holding over a wound in his stomach.

"My God!" Jed said. "All we wanted was to drink a little whiskey and play some cards." He looked over toward the bartender, then toward the other patrons in the saloon. "We didn't want this.. .. We didn't want nothin' like this! Why didn't you folks do somethin' to stop it?"

"Help me, Jed," Wes said. "I'm hurtin' awful bad."

"Frank, come on, let's get him up. We got to get him and Johnny on their horses. We got to get out of here," Jed said.

Suddenly the bat-wing doors to the saloon swung opened, and half-a-dozen commissioners stormed in, all carrying shotguns. The two who had disappeared earlier were with them.

"That's them, that's the two men who started the fight. They murdered Cates and Everly."

"Murdered?" Jed said. "We didn't start no fight, and we didn't murder nobody. It was self-defense."

"We say it was murder."

"Come on, let's take them to Goodwin."

"A hangin'!" someone shouted, rushing into the dining room. "They's gonna be a hangin'!"

The news fell like a bombshell, and everyone in the dining room stood and rushed for the door.

Marcus was as alert to the news as everyone else, but unlike the others, his interest wasn't purely morbid curiosity. "Where's Hank and Bob?" he asked the others at the table.

"Last time I seen 'em, they was makin' the rounds of the saloons," Loomis said. "Shit, if them boys got—uh, pardon ma'am."

Maggie just smiled.

"Come on, let's check on it," Marcus said, leaving Loomis's question unasked. Loomis and Billy Joe started out after Marcus, all three men automatically loosening their pistols.

When they, reached the street, they saw half-a-dozen mounted men. Behind them, hogtied so that they couldn't even stand, were four more men. They were being dragged through the dirt and manure piles in the street. One of the four was badly wounded; another had passed out. The two who were conscious and unhurt were shouting and cursing angrily.

"Let us go, goddamnit! Who the hell are you?"

The commotion had drawn more people than the curious from the hotel dining room. From all over town, saloons and stores were emptying as the good citizens, drawn by the powerful seduction of instant death, poured into the street. Except for the spill of light from the buildings, it was dark, but a couple of men had lit torches and were carrying them as they followed the crowd. The four men were dragged down through the street to the front of the land office building.

"Marcus," Hank said, and Marcus looked around to see that Hank and Bob had joined them.

"You know anything about this?" Marcus asked.

"Just what I heard. The cowboys there got into a shootout in the Royal Flush Saloon and kilt a couple of the commissioners."

"Citizens of Ristine!" Goodwin called, holding his hands up over his head to plead for attention. "Citizens of Ristine, I ask for your attention!"

The crowd, which had been noisy as they followed the parade up the street, now grew quiet.

"Thank you," Goodwin said. "Now, as President of the Commission and the head of this town, I hereby call this court into session."

"Court?" someone shouted from the crowd. "You have the audacity to call this a court?"

"Who is that fella?" Marcus asked one of the towns-people beside him.

"That's G.B. Greer. He's the newspaper editor." Maggie had shown Marcus the newspaper today. He had read with bemused interest the editorial that spoke of the five "riders of destiny" who had arrived in Ristine to show the rest of the town the "courage to stand up to the oppressive commissioners." Marcus had laughed, but he had to admire the courage of a man who would make public his words. Now, Greer was challenging Goodwin again.

"This is a court if I say it's a court," Goodwin answered Greer's charge. "And all your writin' in that newspaper of yours ain't gonna change things. Now, Mr. Fenton, have the prisoners brought before me." Fenton nodded at the commissioners who were with the prisoners, and with a jerk of the ropes, the cowboys were brought before Goodwin. Wes was supported by Jed and Frank. Johnny, who was still passed out, was stretched out in the dirt.

"What's the matter with that prisoner?" Goodwin asked, pointing to the one on the ground.

"Johnny's passed out drunk. He don't even know what's goin' on," Jed said.

"It's better this way," Goodwin said. He looked over at one of the commissioners. "Bailey, you was a witness to the murder?"

"Yes, sir, I was."

"Take a good look at these here men and tell me if they was the ones what did the shootin'."

"They was the ones," Bailey said without moving from his position.

"Goddamnit, I said take a good look. This here court is gonna be fair. Put a torch in front of 'em so's you can see 'em good."

One of the torchbearers held his light in front of the

prisoners. Marcus could see the look of terror in the faces of the cowboys.

"Yes, sir, that was them. We tried to arrest them for being drunk an' disturbin' the peace. They pulled their guns on us and started shootin'."

"You're a lyin' sonofabitch! That ain't true! You started shootin' first, and we was just defendin' ourselves."

"What's your name?"

"Jed Summers."

"You admit you done the shootin'?" Goodwin asked.

"Yeah, we done the shootin', but we was just defendin' ourselves."

"Did the officers try to arrest you?"

"Yeah, but I told 'em we wasn't goin' to no goddamn jail."

"Mr. Summers, you stand convicted by your own testimony," Goodwin said.

"There can be no plea of self-defense when you brutally shoot down an officer of the law while he's doin' his duty. 1 find you all guilty and sentence you to hang."

"What about the one that was drunk?" one of the commissioners asked. "Hang him, too?"

"Him, too. Let justice be done," Goodwin said.

"Justice? This ain't justice, this here is murder!"

"Damn, they gonna hang them men," Hank said.

"Looks like," Marcus said.

"Those sonsofbitches."

Fenton backed a buckboard under a large elm tree that stood in front of the livery stable across the street, then someone tossed four ropes over a big limb that ran at right angles to the tree trunk about fifteen feet above the ground.

Jed, Frank, and Wes were put onto the back of the buckboard and ropes were put around their neck. The man who was passed out drunk was pulled to his feet by the pressure of the rope around his neck. He began gagging and choking, then opened his eyes and looked around, not understanding where he was or what was happening to him.

"You men got 'nything to say?" Goodwin asked.

"Jed?" Johnny asked in a small, frightened voice. Jed was the oldest, and the natural leader of the bunch. "Jed, what's goin' on?"

"We're about to hang, Johhny."

"What are you talkin' about? My God! Jed!" Johnny started screaming, and Goodwin pointed to him.

"Put a gag in that fella's mouth," he ordered.

A rag was stuffed in Johnny's mouth, then a hand-kerchief tied around it to keep it in. Johnny's screams quieted, and he looked on at the proceedings with eyes wide in terror and confusion.

"Jed ... Jed, goddamn ... they really gonna go through with it!" Wes said.

"Take it easy, Wes," Jed said. "Don't let these sonsof-bitches see us afraid."

"What about a preacher?" Frank said. "Don't we get no preacher?"

"Did you give Cates or Everly a chance for a preacher?" Goodwin asked.

"Boys," Jed said. "I've allus heard that if you don't hunch up your shoulders when you drop, you'll die quicker."

"May we all meet on the other side," Frank said in what might have been a prayer.

Goodwin turned to address the crowd. "Let this here hangin' be a lesson to everyone," he shouted. "There is law in Ristine . . . and it will be enforced." He turned to Fenton who was still sitting quietly on the seat of the buckboard. "Mr. Fenton, carry out the sentence."

Fenton snapped the reins, and the team jerked the buckboard forward. The four cowboys were pulled off the back, then they hung from the tree. Johnny and Wes, the wounded cowboy, hung easily, moving back and forth in a slow are caused by the pull of the wagon. Jed and Wes weren't as fortunate. Despite Jed's instructions, the fall didn't break their necks, and they were slowly strangling, lifting their legs and bending at the waist as if in such a way they could take some of the pressure off their neck.

There was a wail of sympathy and indignation from the crowd, but every man present stood glued to the scene by a morbid curiosity.

Marcus stared directly at Quiet Charley Fenton.

Fenton drove the buckboard over to the front of the stable, then got out and began unhitching the team. Not once did he look back toward the four men he had just hanged. It was as if he had simply moved the buckboard from one place to another.

CHAPTER SIX

THE TOWN OF RISTINE, SO WILD AND NOISY THE NIGHT before, was relatively quiet this morning. Marcus and the others stood on the plank walk in front of the Grand Hotel and looked down Main Street at the town.

At the far end of the street, a wagon was pulled up under the hanging tree. The undertaker, a tall, cadaverous man dressed all in black with a high hat, stood beside the wagon, watching. Occasionally he would raise a thin arm and point with a bony finger as he gave directions to his grave digger, a strongly built man who cut down the last of the four cowboys who had been hanged the night before. This was the cowboy who had been wounded in the gunfight, and his chest was covered by blood, dried now to a reddish brown. His body was laid out in the wagon with the other three. From there they would be taken to the hardware store where a back room served as a mortuary.

There, they would join four more bodies already in pine coffins. The gambler Hank killed, the three killed in the shootout, and the four men hanged made a total of eight men who would be buried today.

"What I don't understand is why these folks stay around and put up with all this," Loomis said. "Why don't they just leave town?"

"Cause there's money to be made in this town," Marcus answered. "Ever'one figures the railroad comin' to town's gonna make 'em rich."

Bob chuckled. "Seems to me like the only one gettin' rich 'round here is the undertaker."

"How 'bout us, Marcus?" Hank asked. "Any money in this town for us?"

"Hell, I told you, I'm gonna win that horse race next Saturday," Loomis said.

Marcus smiled. "Yeah, but Hank's right, Loomis. If there's this many people tryin' to get their hands on it, then there's bound to be some for us."

"Yeah, well, in the meantime I'm going to find another poker game," Hank said.

Bob, Loomis, and Billy Joe went with Hank, leaving Marcus on his own. As Marcus walked down the street, the tranquility of the morning was suddenly shattered by a loud crashing noise in the building just in front of him. A large box came flying through the door, landed in the street, then broke open and scattered its contents in the dirt. G.B. Greer, a smallish, balding man, wearing an ink-stained apron, ran out of the newspaper office into the street and knelt down in the dirt to begin picking up the scattered type.

"Just leave it there, Greer!" a gruff voice called. Three more men came out of the newspaper office. They were all wearing badges, and one of them was carrying a shotgun.

"I can't leave it here," Greer complained. "How will I get out my paper?"

"This here trash is worse'n what you did yesterday. Mr. Goodwin's a patient man, but he ain't gonna put up with this," the man said, holding a wadded-up page in his hand.'

"Every word is the truth," the newspaper man said. "Those men were hanged without a trial."

"They had a trial."

"That was a mockery of justice."

"Yeah, well, that's the only justice the people in this town are gonna get." The speaker, the one with the shotgun, kicked the box, scattering the type for the second time. Greer started picking it up again.

"I said leave it." He cocked his shotgun, and at the sound of the hammers being pulled back, the newspaper man stood up. He was shaking with fear and rage.

"Look at that little fella shake, Eugene," one of the commissioners said. Eugene was the one with the shotgun. "Ever seen a fella shake like that?"

"Bet he's about to pee in his pants," Eugene said. "Haw! Wouldn't that be' a sight."

"Please," Greer said to the few who had gathered around to watch. "Someone help me." He saw Marcus. "You! You're one of those I wrote about in my editorial yesterday. You aren't afraid of these people. Please help me."

"You plannin' on gettin' involved, mister?" Eugene asked.

"This ain't none of my business," Marcus answered.

Eugene smiled broadly and lowered the hammers on the shotgun. "Well, now, glad to see your're on our side."

"He didn't say he was on our side, Eugene. He said it weren't none of his business."

"The way I look at it," Eugene went on, "he's either for us, or ag'in us. Right, mister?"

By now a dozen onlookers had gathered to watch, and twice that many people were being drawn to the scene, hurrying down the boardwalk, rushing across the street, spilling out of the stores and saloons. Marcus started to walk away.

"Hey, you!" Eugene called after him. "I asked you a question. You ain't answered me yet."

"I'd let it be, mister," Marcus said.

The smile left Eugene's face. "Maybe you ain't gettin' the whole picture here." He patted the breech with his hand a couple of times. "Now, if you want to be friendly, answer the question."

Marcus sighed. It had gone the limit now ... he knew a killing was about to take place. He felt no hot rush of blood, no fear. He felt only a deadly calm and an absolute assurance that he would come out on top. "Have it your way, mister."

Eugene grinned broadly. "Well, now, I was wonderin' what it would take to get through to you." Marcus looked down at the street at the type still scattered in the dirt, then he looked back at Eugene. Engene was still smiling, cocksure of himself.

"Your name is Eugene?"

"Yeah."

"Eugene, help pick up the type," Marcus ordered quietly.

The crowd of onlookers was large now, and there was a collective gasp as they realized what Marcus said.

Eugene laughed a short, ugly laugh.

"Mister, you talk just like'n you took leave of your senses."

"You tell 'im, Eugene!"

"Yeah, gut-shoot the bastard!"

"I ain't gonna tell you again," Marcus said. "Pick up the type."

"Mister, please, I'm sorry I got you into it. I don't want no more trouble," Greer said. "I'll pick up my own type."

"No, you won't," Marcus said. "Eugene here is goin' to pick up your type."

"Mister, you got more nerve and less sense than anyone I ever run across in my life," Eugene said to Marcus.

"My name's Marcus. Marcus Quinn."

That s'posed to mean somethin' to me?"

"I don't reckon," Marcus said. "I just thought you might want to know the name of the man that's gonna kill you."

"What?" Eugene gasped, and though he was holding the shotgun and Marcus was standing there with his hands empty, there was something about Marcus's voice, something cold and dry, like the rattling of bones in a graveyard. Despite himself, Eugene felt a quick stab of fear shoot through him.

"Pick up the type or die with that gun in your hands," Marcus said coldly.

"Shoot 'im, Eugene. Shoot 'im!" one of the other commissioners said anxiously.

Eugene forced himself to smile; then he started to thumb back the hammers on his double-barrel. He didn't even get them half-cocked before Marcus had his Colt in his hand. There was a snap of primer cap, then a roar of exploding powder, though both events happened so quickly as to be one loud bang. A finger of flame shot from the end of the Colt. Eugene dropped his shotgun and grabbed his chest. His eyes opened wide in pain and shock. He fell against the doorjamb of the newspaper office, then slid down to the sidewalk, leaving a smear of blood on the wall behind him. He wound up in the sitting position, his eyes open and blank.

"My God, did you see that?" someone in the crowd

asked. "This feller just kilt Eugene with Eugene holdin' a gun in his hand."

"I ain't never seen anyone that fast."

Marcus looked at the other two commissioners. Neither of them had drawn, having felt secure by the fact that Eugene had a shotgun in the ready position.

Shooting Eugene had been easy, but only someone with Marcus's experience would realize that. Marcus had looked deep into Eugene's eyes and knew he would stop and think before he actually pulled the trigger of his scatter gun. While he was thinking about it, Marcus would be acting, and drawing and shooting for someone with Marcus's speed was one step, not two.

"Pick up the type," Marcus ordered coldly.

'Yes, sir," one of the two remaining commissioners mumbled.

"No, get away from me, all of you!" the newspaper man shouted. "I'll pick up my own damn type." Marcus looked at Greer for a moment, then put his pistol back in his holster. As he walked away, he could feel the two commissioner's eyes boring holes in his back. He knew they were too afraid to draw.

An hour later the two commissioners reported the fight to Barlow Goodwin.

Goodwin pulled an expensive cigar from the humidor on his desk, licked along the edge, then lit the end. He puffed several times, blowing out clouds of blue smoke, examining his deputies through the smoke. Finally, he spoke.

"Let me get this straight," he said. "You say there were three of you, all armed. Eugene had the drop on Quinn, and yet he still killed him."

"That's what happened."

Goodwin studied the fire on the end of his cigar for a moment. "All right, you told me. Now what do you expect me to do about it?"

"Send the albino after him."

Fenton, who had been sitting quietly listening to the conversation, looked toward the speaker. His eyes and face remained cold and expressionless, but the very fact that his head had moved . . . like the head of a snake watching its victim before it strikes . . . had an unnerving effect.

"Tell me, Gilmore, are you talking about Mr. Fenton?"

Gilmore cleared his throat. "Yeah," he said. "Well, I didn't mean nothin' by callin' him a albino. I just meant..."

Fenton looked away. He'd already lost interest in Gilmore.

"Never mind," Goodwin said. "Mr. Fenton didn't take offense."

"Good," Gilmore mumbled.

"Only thing," the other commissioner suggested; "if Fenton does take out after this fella, he ought to take four, maybe five men with him."

"You, for one, Tanner?"

"Well, I'd ... uh ... go after Quinn, iffen there was enough of us. But don't forget they's five of'em."

"Yes, there are five," Goodwin said.

"I wouldn't want to go after 'em 'less we had 'em at least doubled."

"That's real brave of you, Tanner," Goodwin said. "But it won't be necessary. I'm sure Mr. Fenton could take care of him by himself."

"If you think the albino's faster'n this fella, you're crazy!" Gilmore said quickly. "I seen Fenton work, and I seen this fella."

Goodwin shook his head. "Fast? Who said anything about fast? If Mr. Fenton takes care of the job, fast will have nothing to do with it. Killing isn't a game with Mr. Fenton. It's a business." Goodwin looked toward the albino. "And I think it time he goes to work." Without a word, Fenton got up and started for the door.

"On second thought," Goodwin called, out, and Fenton stopped. "Let me speak with Mr. Quinn first." Fenton turned and went back to his chair. He sat down again, his face as expressionless now as it had been when he stood up.

By now nearly everyone had a story to tell about the five strangers who had ridden into town yesterday, the men G.B. Greer had called "riders of destiny." How the youngest and smallest of the group had taken out two men with a swift kick and a chair within moments after they arrived. How Hank went up against a Remington with a peppergun, how Bob had cut the clothes from the back of three men with his bullwhip, how Marcus had killed Eugene even as Eugene held a shotgun in his hands.

A bunch of merchants strained their brains to see if anyone had ever heard of them, at their daily meeting in front of the general store. One man said that he seemed to remember an outfit like that from the war ... a group that rode with Quantrill.

"Quinn's Raiders!" another said, snapping his fingers as he recalled stories about them. "Only they didn't ride with Quantrill, they was on their own, and they made Quantrill's bunch seem like preachers."

"Can't be them.... They was kilt when a railroad car blew up while they was bein' took to prison."

"They never found their bodies."

"They didn't find no bodies a-tall. Could be they got out."

"You think that's really them?"

"Yeah. I seen 'em once. I know'd yesterday I'd seen 'em before, somewhere."

"If we're smart, we won't say nothin' about this to 'em. Might make 'em mad, and I don't know about you men, I sure as hell don't want 'em mad at me."

"I fought for the Union, an' I never thought I'd be on the side of a group of Rebel raiders. But damn if I wouldn't like to see them boys take the commissioners down a notch or two."

"Hell, we won't tell none of the commissioners what

we know, either. This might prove to be real interestin'
to watch."

When Marcus joined Hank and the others, he saw
that they were all sitting together at the same table.
Bob, using his foot, pushed out a fifth chair for their
leader.

"I thought you were going to play some cards,"
Marcus said.

"Yeah," Hank said. 'I thought so, too."

"What happened?"

"Funny thing, ever'time I sit down at a table,
ever'one that's playin' already suddenly remembers
some chore they forgot."

"Bad enough when Hank kilt that fella yesterday,
then Bob come cut up a couple more with his bullwhip," Loomis said. "Now, you've gone an' kilt one.
Ever'one's afraid of us."

"Maybe not everyone," Marcus suggested, and' he
nodded toward the door."

Barlow Goodwin had just stepped through the bat-
wing doors of the saloon. When he saw Marcus and the
others sitting around the table, he held his jacket open
wide to show that he wasn't armed and walked over.

"Mr. Quinn?"

"That's me."

"You do remember me, don't you, Mr. Quinn? We
met yesterday."

"Yeah," Marcus said. "I know who you are."

"I'd like to talk to you."

"We're listening," Marcus invited.

"What I've got to say is private. Please join me in my private rooms out back."

The Raiders followed Goodwin to the back where he had his private office.

"You boys haven't exactly been quiet since you come into town," he said after they'd sat down.

"I reckon that's true."

"How long you planning to stay?"

"As long as we goddamn well want," Quinn said. Goodwin cleared his throat.

"Please don't get me wrong. I wasn't suggesting that I want you men to leave."

"That's good," Hawk said. "Wouldn't be neighborly."

"I'm inclined to agree," Goodwin said.

"We're gonna at least stay past the race," Loomis said.

"The race?"

"The horse race this Saturday. I plan to ride in it."

"For the money?"

"Not for the fun."

"I see. You boys interested in money?"

"Yeah."

"Tell me, would you men be interested in workin' for me? The pay is good."

"How good?" Marcus asked.

"More than you can win in that race," Goodwin said.

"Keep talkin'."

"I need someone to help keep a little order around here."

"You mean you want us to join that group of pissants you got wearin' badges?"

"Actually, they're commissioners," Goodwin corrected.

"Yeah, well, whatever the hell you call them, we ain't interested."

"I really didn't think you would be interested in wearing tin badges," Goodwin said. He looked around the room conspiratorially. "But maybe you'd be interested in bein' in on some real money."

"You mean railroad money?"

"In a manner of speakin', yes. You see, I'm in the business of sellin' plots of land alongside the right of way. Land like that can make a fella rich."

"None of us are interested in stayin' in one place long enough to wait for that kind of land to pay off," Marcus said.

Goodwin smiled. "Neither am I, my friend," he said. "The only money that's gonna be made outta the land that's sold here in town is the money that's bein' made now."

"What do you mean?"

"The railroad ain't exactly comin' through Ristine," Goodwin said. "It's goin' about ten miles south of here. It means waitin' a while for that land to get real valuable, but it won't be long. In the meantime... there's good, quick money to be made right here in town, if you're willin' to go along with me.

"What exactly did you have in mind?" Marcus asked.

Goodwin stroked his mustache for a moment, then leaned back in his chair. "When the time is right, I intend to tell the good people of Ristine that the railroad has changed its mind and is rerouting the line. I'll offer to sell them new tracts of land ... at a handsome profit, of course ... but there may be some people who won't like that. They might try and do something about it. If they do ... I'd like to think that you boys were on my side."

"What about your commissioners?" Hank asked. "You got enough of them working for you. Don't you think they could handle the problem?"

Goodwin smiled a small, conspiratorial smile. "Well, they may be a part of the problem," he said. "Say what?" Billy Joe asked.

"He means the commissioners don't know any more about the real route of the railroad than the folks in town," Marcus said. "Am I right, Goodwin?"

"Yes."

"And you sold them right-of-way property at reduced rates?"

"I paid for their services with land," Goodwin said. "Only Mr. Fenton knows otherwise."

"Seems like you took quite a chance," Marcus suggested.

"Yes, I suppose so. When the time was right, I intended to take a few of the more trusted and competent commissioners into my confidence. I figured they could handle the others. But now that I have seen the way you men work, I'm sure you would be much more effective. What about it, do you want in?"

"How much money?" Marcus asked.

"By the time we're all through here, I'd say..."

"No. I mean, how much money now?" Marcus asked. "Cash ... in advance."

"Suppose ... suppose I give you a thousand dollars now," Goodwin said. "That's two hundred dollars apiece..."

"We can cipher," Loomis said quickly.

Goodwin cleared his throat nervously.

"Yes, of course. All right, suppose I give you two hundred dollars apiece right now and another two hundred dollars apiece when your work is finished?"

"You just want protection from the commissioners when they find out, right? No hangings, no gunplay."

"No, just take care of the commissioners."

"What do you boys think?" Marcus asked.

"A couple thousand is pretty good money," Hank said.

"And I sure as hell don't like the commissioners," Bob put in. "Ain't like we're bein' asked to do somethin' we don't want to do anyway."

"And that would give us more money to bet on the race," Loomis put in.

Without being asked, Marcus reached over and took the cigar Goodwin was fingering nervously. He lit it before he spoke.

"You know, I heard of people robbin' with a gun," he said. "But you're the first one I've ever known that could rob with a fountain pen." He smiled, though the smile went only skin deep. "I reckon one way's about as good as another. Count out the money, Goodwin. We got a deal."

CHAPTER SEVEN

IT WAS AFTER DARK BY THE TIME MARCUS RETURNED TO the hotel for dinner. He was met by Helga as he stepped into the dining room.

"Good evening, Mr. Quinn," she greeted.

"Hello, Helga. What's good for supper?"

"Your supper, you will not eat here," she said.

"Oh? Where'm I supposed to eat it?"

Helga smiled at him, then walked over to a glassed-in sideboy along the wall. She took a bottle of whiskey from behind a large platter, then poured a glass and brought it over to Marcus.

"Is Tennessee sour mash," she said. "Miss Pettibone said maybe you will like."

Marcus took a sip, then let out a long, low sigh of appreciation. It had been a long, long time since he had tasted sipping whiskey this good.

"Yes," he said. "This is fine whiskey."

The whiskey reminded Marcus of the days in Mississippi before the war when all he had on his mind was women, drink, and fun. That was when he and the others came together for the first time. Marcus, Hank, Billy Joe, and the Depro brothers were the scourge of Mississippi, and there wasn't a bordello, whiskey still, or county sheriff they didn't know, intimately.

That all seemed so long ago now, so removed from the life he had lived for the past several years, that it was almost as if it had happened to someone else. Since the days of the Tennessee sour mash and Kentucky bourbon, he had drunk in saloons that were no more than a board plank laid across two empty barrels, the whiskey so green that it had to be colored with rusty nails and flavored with chewing tobacco.

"Mr. Quinn, Miss Pettibone said one glass of this you should drink, then go to her room. There, your dinner she will serve."

"All right," Marcus said, taking another swallow. "Sounds fine to me." He looked around the dining room and saw that Billy Joe was sitting alone at a table in the back of the room. Then, as he looked closer, he saw that though Billy Joe was alone, there was another setting across the table from him. He looked pointedly at the setting, then at Helga, and Helga blushed.

"Yeah," she said. "I am with Billy Joe, eating my supper."

"Good for Billy Joe," Marcus said. He finished the

whiskey, then sat the glass on the table and left the dining room to go up the stairs to the second floor.

The top floor of the Grand Hotel was constructed in a large U, with the base of the U being the landing that overlooked the lobby below. A hallway going down each side formed the legs of the U. Rooms opened off either side of the hallway, and Maggie's room was at the far end of the right leg. The hallway was supposed to be lighted by four gas lanterns, but only one of the lanterns was burning, so that the hallway was dark.

Marcus walked past the brown doors that led into each of the rooms until he came to the last door on the right. He tapped once lightly, and the door opened.

"Good evening, Mr. Marcus Quinn," Maggie's husky voice said. She was wearing a black chemise and nothing more. The nipples of her breasts protruded through the silk, and Marcus reached up to touch them. They grew harder, and Maggie shuddered once, then slipped the chemise over her shoulders and let it fall to the floor. Now, completely naked, she leaned up against him, then reached down to touch the bulge in front of Marcus's pants. She began opening the buttons. A second later Marcus felt his organ free as she pulled it out.

"Please do not think, Mr. Marcus Quinn, that I meet everyone in this way," Maggie said. Her long, cool fingers moved across his organ. She kissed him, and her tongue came out serpentlike to dart into his mouth.

She raised one leg to the side of his hip and took him inside her.

Marcus was taken completely by surprise, and as his knees weakened, he had to lean back against the wall on the opposite side of the hall from her door. He put his hands down to her hips, not to push her away, but to move her to him. As she hunched against him, his mouth moved down across her naked shoulders to her distended nipples. He bit them gently, and flicked his tongue against them.

Marcus heard one of the doors close down the hall and realized at that moment that they were out in the hall in plain view. If anyone came down to this end of the hall they would be in for quite a surprise. Thinking about that, he gently tried to push her back so he could step the rest of the way inside, at least far enough to close the door.

"No," she whispered into his ear. She continued to hump against him. "No, I don't want to stop ... not for a minute ... not even for a second."

Marcus started to explain the situation to her, but the sensations were too strong. He smiled. To hell with it. If it didn't bother her, it didn't bother him. He stood there, letting her have her way with him until he rocked back on his heels and shuddered, then put his hands on her ass and pulled her tightly against him. Finally, long moments after the last tremors were gone, Maggie dropped her leg and pulled away. She smiled at him.

"Oh," she said. "Where are my manners? Won't you please come in?"

The dinner had been eaten, and Marcus was enjoying a glass of wine and a good cigar. He was relaxed, more relaxed than he had been at any time since coming to Ristine.

"Maggie, how much money you got invested with Goodwin?" he asked.

"Well, like I told you, I bought a big lot," she said. "I plan to build a hotel for the railroad guests."

"There won't be any."

"Maybe at first, but I figure that after a while . . ."

"No," Marcus interrupted. "There won't be any railroad guests ... because there won't be any railroad."

"What. . . what are you talking about? Of course there's going to be a railroad. Why, everyone knows that. There's a map that shows the route and everything."

Marcus shook his head slowly. "No," he said. "The railroad is going to bypass Ristine."

Maggie looked at Marcus for a long, quite moment before she spoke again.

"When did you find that out?"

"Today."

"I don't understand. What made them change their mind?"

"They didn't change their mind. They never planned to come through here in the first place. This was all a scheme cooked up by Barlow Goodwin."

Maggie gasped. "What? You mean he has cheated all these people? The whole town?"

Marcus chuckled. "He's cheated you, Maggie. What are you worried about everyone else for?"

Maggie was quiet for a long moment. "How did you find out?" she asked.

"He told me. He wants the boys and me to protect him from the commissioners when he breaks the news."

"You mean he cheated them, too?"

"Yep."

Suddenly and inexplicably, Maggie laughed out loud. "The commissioners . . . the high and mighty defenders of justice . . . cheated like the rest of us."

Maggie laughed until her sides hurt, then she leaned back and wiped her eyes.

"You know something? It's almost worth getting cheated to know that they are getting theirs." She looked at Marcus. "What I don't understand is, why are you telling me?"

"I figure we can get your money back."

"Oh, I don't know," Maggie said. "I wouldn't feel right asking him to give my money back knowing all the while that there were so many people in town who had been cheated, too."

Marcus chuckled. "Don't get me wrong," he said. "I wasn't planning on *asking* the sonofabitch to give you back your money. ... I was planning on taking enough of it that your share would pay you back." Maggie's eyes grew wide in surprise; then they flashed with quick laughter.

"Take it from him? You mean cheat him out of it ... or steal it from him?"

"That's the best way," Marcus said.

Maggie clapped her hands together once and let out a squeal of delight. "Yes!" she said. "Yes, now that I would enjoy doing."

The next morning Loomis stood on the back stoop of the hotel. The grass was still covered with early morning dew, and it caused hundreds of prisms to catch the sunlight, then split it into all the colors of the rainbow. Half a block down the street, a rooster crowed, then another, still farther away, answered the challenge. Next door to the hotel, the back door of a small house opened, and a woman tossed out a pan of water.

Loomis stretched, then walked out back of the hotel to the stable so he could check on the horses. Quinn's Raiders had been to town for nearly a week now, and Loomis had gone out to the stable every day to see to the feeding and exercise of their mounts. This morning, as he approached the barn, he saw a man nailing a poster to the corral gate.

FOURTH OF JULY CELEBRATION
FIREWORKS PICNIC
and

HORSE RACING
featuring
JASON PENDARROW
and his champion quarter horse
DANCER
Race to be held at 2:00 PM in
RISTINE, NEVADA
Sponsored by the Kansas and Pacific RR

"Is this the race this Saturday that poster's talkin' about?" Loomis asked.

"Yes, sir, it sure is."

"I knew about the race," Loomis said. "I didn't know anyone was comin' in from some other place to ride in it. Who is this fella?"

"Jason Pendarrow? Why, he's the best rider there is. And his horse is a champion. They say he's never lost a race. More'n ten thousand people showed up to watch him race in St. Louis back in May."

Loomis had heard about a professional rider, an Englishman with a champion horse who toured the country racing all comers and beating them in such places as Chicago, St. Louis, Kansas City, Denver, and San Francisco.

"This fella a foreigner?"

"Sure is. You have heard of him, huh?"

"I reckon I have," Loomis said. "But why he'd come to Ristine? I thought he only raced in the big cities."

"Well, I reckon someone made it worth his while to come to Ristine," the man with the posters said.

"What if he don't win?"

The man putting out the posters laughed. "Why, they ain't no chance that he won't win. Who could beat him?"

"Me, maybe," Loomis said.

"You really believe that?"

"Ain't nothin' go on forever. Somebody's gonna beat him one of these days," Loomis said. "Might as well be me."

"I'll give you this. You're a wiry little fella. It's been my notice that them's the kind that does best. Well, good luck to you. I got a lot more of these things to put out."

Loomis watched the man leave carrying a large bundle of posters under his arm. Half a block away, he began putting up another one.

Loomis tore the poster off, then took it back into the kitchen with him, still studying it. It wasn't the rider that bothered him, it was the horse. Dancer was said to be a fine horse, bred for racing. He was kept for racing only, tended to full time by a trainer who did nothing but feed and exercise him. On the other hand, the horse Loomis would ride in the race was the same horse he had ridden into town. All things considered, it no longer seemed like a sure thing to him that he would win on Saturday.

"Hello," a young woman's voice said.

When Loomis looked up from the poster he was carrying, he saw Penny. Penny was the youngest and one of the most popular of the girls working at the hotel. Loomis had noticed her, though he had never visited her, because her nights always seemed busy, and he had no desire to wait in line.

"Howdy," Loomis answered.

"I saw you from my window," Penny said. When Loomis didn't answer, she went on. "I see you every morning. You go out to check the horses; sometimes you exercise them."

"Yes."

"Are you in charge of the horses for you an' all your friends?"

"I guess so," Loomis said.

"Why?"

"It just sort of works out that way," he said. "I like horses... I'm the best with them, I guess."

"I like horses, too," Penny said. "When 1 lived in Kentucky, my father raised horses."

"There are some good horses in Kentucky," Loomis agreed.

"I've got some coffee brewing if you want some."

"Thanks. What are you doing up so early, anyway? I thought all you girls slept until noon."

Penny smiled. "Sometimes I take a nap in the afternoons, but I like to get up early. I've always thought this was the best time of the day."

"Yeah," Loomis said. "I like early morning, too." Penny poured the coffee for both of them, then sat down and indicated that he should join her. She smiled almost shyly at him as she picked up her cup.

"You ain't ever come to see me," she said. "I kept thinkin' maybe you'd be the next one to come through my door, but you ain't never done it."

Loomis blew on the coffee to cool it, then he slurped it between extended lips before he answered.

"No, I reckon I haven't."

"Don't you think I'm pretty?"

"Yeah," Loomis said. "I think you're one of the prettiest girls I ever seen. But I don't... uh, my brother, he's the one that..."

"You don't like whores, is that it?"

"I got nothin' personal again't you. It's just that I don't think it's somethin' you ought to pay for. Seems to me like it's more personal."

"Loomis, don't you know I wouldn't charge you nothin'?"

"You wouldn't?"

"We're just like anyone else," she said. "If we find a man we take a cotton to, why, we can be with him. Look at Miss Pettibone an' your friend, Quinn. 'Course she ain't really no line girl, but she is the boss lady, so in a way it's the same thing."

"It ain't just the payin'," Loomis said. "I don't like

standin' in line, waitin' my turn, then climbin' into a saddle some other man's done soaped up."

Penny took in a short intake of breath, then blinked her eyes several times and stared into her coffee cup. Despite her efforts to prevent it, tears formed at the comers of her eyes, then streaked down her cheek.

Loomis was surprised when he saw that, and he reached up and touched her cheek, gently catching one of her tears with the end of his finger. "I'm sorry, girl," he said quietly. "I didn't mean to hurt your feelin's none, little lady."

"That's all right," Penny said. "They ain't nobody holdin' me in the life. I'm doin' it all on my own."

They were silent for a long moment, the only sound being the pop and snap of a fire in the kitchen wood stove and the clink of the coffee cups as they set them in their saucers.

"Yes." Penny's cheeks flamed in embarrassment. "I ain't sorry, mind. I am what I am, and I reckon I'll stand by it. The money is good. And when the man is nice and gentle, I'd be lyin' to you if I told you I didn't like it. In fact. . . it's down right pleasurable." She smiled. "Sometimes, I see a man I like, and I think about what it would be like to be with him. Like with you."

Loomis took a sip of his coffee and looked at Penny. "I ain't never gonna stand in line, but if you hear a knock on your door in the afternoon when you takin' your nap ... get up and open it. You might find that it's me."

Penny smiled broadly. "Why, Loomis Depro, you won't even have to knock."

Penny watched Loomis and his friends ride out together late that afternoon. She had no idea where they were going, or when they would be back, or even if they would be back. She didn't have long to wonder about it, though, because the business started early that evening.

It was after 1:00 A.M. when her last visitor left, a young drover from a nearby ranch who, though awkward and shy, had been nice to her. In age and manner, he reminded her of Loomis, and as she lay on her bed alone, she thought of him. She very much wanted him to come visit her. He might be the same age as the young drover who just left, but she knew he would be a skilled lover. She didn't know how she knew... She just knew.

There was another knock on her door. At first she was surprised because it had been several minutes since her last visitor, and the quietness of the house indicated that the evening's business was through. Then she realized it must be Loomis, and with a broad smile she hopped up from her bed and rushed over to open the door. When she saw who was on the other side, her smile left her lips.

Quiet Charley Fenton stood out in the hall, his pale skin even paler in the dim light of the hall lamp. His pink eyes glowed obscenely, and without saying a word, he stepped inside.

Penny shuddered. She had entertained him before. . . . She knew what he was like, and she didn't want any part of him. But she had no choice.

"Take off the gown," Fenton grunted as he began stripping out of his own clothes, exposing even more of his pale skin. To Penny, he looked like a white grub worm turned up by rolling over a log.

Penny decided that the best thing to do would be to satisfy him as quickly as possible, hoping he would then leave. She slipped the gown over her head, then stood nude before him. He reached out for one of her nipples. She closed her eyes and braced herself for what she knew was coming next.

Maggie was just getting ready for bed when she heard Penny cry out. She was a little surprised, she thought all the men were gone. Then, when she heard Penny again, she realized that it was a cry of fear and pain, and she knew that it had to be Fenton. She had seen him earlier hanging around in the parlor downstairs. She had kept an eye on him, but he disappeared, and she thought he had left. Now, she knew that he hadn't.

Maggie stepped out into the hall and hurried down toward Penny's room. She heard another muffled cry, and the hate and anger boiled up inside her. When she reached the door to Penny's room, she threw it open without even bothering to knock. Penny was lying on her bed, her skin already covered with marks where Fenton had abused her. Even now, he was squeezing one of her nipples between his thumb and forefinger, squeezing it so tightly that it had swollen to the size and color of a ripe cherry.

"You!" Maggie said angrily, pointing at Fenton. "Get out of here!"

"You get out," Fenton said. "I paid for this whore."

"You didn't pay to torture her!" Maggie picked up a water pitcher and started toward him. Holding his arms up to shield himself, he moved quickly away from Penny's bed.

"You had better watch out," Fenton hissed.

"Me watch out?" Maggie shouted angrily. "You are the one who better watch out! You and your thieving, cheating boss! You're going to get yours, all of you!" Without another word, Fenton started putting on his clothes. He stepped into his pants, then pulled on his boots and strapped on his gun. While he was getting dressed, Maggie went over to look at Penny, who was lying in bed whimpering in pain.

"Oh, you poor thing," Maggie said, looking at the welts on the young girl's body. She looked over at Fenton, her eyes flashing hate and anger at him. "How could you do something like this?"

"She is a whore," Fenton said. "It don't matter what you do to a whore."

"Get out of here! Get out of here now and never come back, you maggot!"

Fenton's eyes narrowed until they were but two, pink slits in a pasty white face.

"I don't take to that none," he said.

"Maggot!" Maggie screamed. "Maggot!" She picked up the water pitcher and threw it at him, causing it to crash into slivers of glass on the wall behind him. One sliver nicked his face, and a bright red line of blood started oozing down his cheek.

Coldly and without another word, Fenton pulled his gun and shot her. The shot was so loud and sudden that it blotted out all that had gone on before. Maggie grabbed her throat and looked at Fenton as if unable to believe that he had shot her. She fell back against the bed, then slid down to the floor. Her head fell back on the bed, and she blinked a couple of times, then died.

"Maggie!" Penny sobbed. "My God, Maggie!" "Crazy woman," Fenton said, wiping the blood from his cheek. "She tried to kill me."

The size of Maggie Pettibone's funeral would probably have surprised her. She had been a schoolteacher in St. Louis and figured to live a lonely life, probably die an old maid, and be buried quietly in some city cemetery with no more than a few teachers to note her passing. In Ristine her passing was noted by half the town. Marcus and the boys were among those present at the funeral, standing quietly in the background while the preacher laid her in the grave.

When the original owner of the Grand Hotel had been shot, the will that left the hotel to Maggie specified that the hotel be kept open and business go on as usual on the day of her funeral. Maggie had made the same arrangements in her own will, leaving the hotel to Helga with the provision that business go on as usual. As a result the hotel stayed open, and Helga invited the boys back for dinner.

"Self-defense," Hank snarled in disgust at the table. "Barlow held that court of his and ruled that Fenton killed Maggie in self-defense."

"Marcus, we ain't gonna let that bastard get away with it, are we?" Loomis asked.

Marcus had been unusually quiet from the moment they had returned to town and learned of the murder.

"Yeah, Marcus," Billy Joe put in. "Ain't right."

Marcus looked at the others around the table. "I don't know 'bout you, but I figure Barlow's got to pay same as Fenton. Barlow's the one that brought him to town in the first place, and Barlow's the one let him off."

"What you got in mind?" Bob asked.

"We're gonna take all the sonofabitch's money. And Fenton?" He let the words hang for a moment.

"What about Fenton?" Hank asked.

"That milk-faced bastard's going to die," Marcus said easily.

CHAPTER EIGHT

GREER KNEW THAT HIS LATEST ARTICLE HAD HIT HOME, because when he came to work that morning, he found his newspaper office vandalized once again. The type, however, hadn't been scattered. After the incident the other day, when a commissioner was shot down right in front of the newspaper office, Greer began taking the type boxes home with him. With no type to scatter, the vandals had turned the press over on its side. He sat it back up, then went about tightening and adjusting the components that had been loosened by the tumble. When Hank Proudy stepped through the door of the newspaper office later that morning, he saw the editor on his knees with a screwdriver working on his press.

"You havin' a problem?"

"Would you hold the tympanum for me while I tighten it?" Greer asked, pointing to the item so Hank would know what he was talking about.

Hank held the hinged wooden cover while the adjustment was made.

"The Washington hand press is perhaps the sturdiest press ever built," the editor explained. "But even it requires a modicum of maintenance when it is pushed over. There, that should do it."

Greer stood up, moved the tympanum over the bed, and raised it up half-a-dozen times to test it. Then he wiped his hands on his apron and looked at Hank.

"Seems to me like you spend most of your time just cleanin' up the mess people cause."

"Freedom of the press isn't free," Greer said. "I know you. You're a friend of Quinn's, aren't you?"

"I reckon I am."

"I'm glad whoever tipped over the press was gone. If he had still been here, I imagine you would have wanted to shoot him."

"Well, now, Mr. Editor ..."

"The name's Greer. G.B. Greer."

"Instead of bein' so critical, you might be thankful to Marcus."

"Thankful? For watching a man be killed on my account? I could've picked up the type; nobody needed to be killed."

"You talk like Marcus shot him for no reason at all."

"If you mean did the other fella have a gun out, I'll admit that. But Quinn could have avoided the fight."

"By coming in here and wrecking more of your paper."

Greer looked around the newspaper office for a moment, then sighed and shook his head.

"All right," he finally admitted. "You're right. I guess I was conducting such a crusade against violence that I overlooked the fact that an occasional act of violence is a necessary tool on the side of right. After all, what was the Revolutionary War . . . the War between the States, if not acts of violence?"

"Like you said, Mr. Greer, freedom of the press don't come free."

"I apologize for my outburst, mister. Now, what can I do for you?"

"This newspaper print advertisements?"

"Of course we do, sir. That is fully one-half of my source of revenue."

"Good," Hank said. He pulled a piece of paper from his pocket and handed it to the editor. "I want you to print this."

Attention to all who desire to place a wager on the horse race to be held in Ristine at 2:00 PM on July 4.1 shall be betting on Loomis Depro to win and will take all bets. See Hank Proudy, Grand Hotel.

"It'll be a pleasure to print something pleasant for a change," Greer said. "Yes, sir. I, for one, am looking forward to the celebration Saturday. But are you sure you want to cover all bets on Pendarrow?"

"I'm sure."

"You ever see Pendarrow or his horse before?"

"Nope."

Greer chuckled. "Well, friend, I hope you have enough money to cover your losses."

"Is Pendarrow that good?"

"He's the best," Greer said.

"Then it should be a good race."

"You still want to run this?"

"Yep."

Greer laid the note down, then began assembling type. "All right, that'll be one dollar," he said.

"Did you get the notice in the newspaper?" Marcus asked a little later.

"Sure did," Hank answered. "I also got some advice that I not waste my money by betting on Loomis."

"The editor was concerned about it, was he?"

"Says Pendarrow is the best there is."

"Good. Now, let's go see Mr. Goodwin about a little business proposition," Marcus said.

As the two men walked from the hotel to the Land Commission office, they saw the extent to which the little town of Ristine was getting ready to celebrate the holiday. Though the holiday was still two days away, the entire street was decked out in red, white, and blue bunting.

"Since Vicksburg the Fourth of July hasn't meant much to me," Hank said.

"I know what you mean," Marcus said. Vicksburg had finally succumbed to Yankee siege on the Fourth of July, 1863. Though neither of the boys was in the city at the time, both had relatives who lived there, and both had been fighting for the South when they heard the news. Mississippi, their home state, had not celebrated the Fourth of July since that date, and the boys knew the folks at home wouldn't be celebrating it this year, either. "But, we ain't in Mississippi anymore," he went on.

"Yeah. Don't I know it."

Four commissioners were standing in front of the Land Commission office when Marcus and Hank reached it, and they moved in such a way as to block the entrance. They recognized Hank and Marcus as the same two men who had killed two of their own, and the look they were giving them now showed that their presence was anything but welcome.

"What do you two want here?"

"We come to see Goodwin," Marcus said.

Quiet Charley Fenton appeared in the door of the office then and with a small nod indicated that the commissioners should let Marcus and Hank come in.

"Mr. Quinn," Goodwin said. "I thought our . . . uh . . . arrangement, would best be served by our not being seen together."

"This has nothing to do with the arrangement," Marcus said.

"Then, why are you here?"

"Money."

"Money? See here, Quinn, we agreed ..."

Marcus waved his hand. "No, not that," he said. "I have a proposition. A sure thing. Are you interested?"

"I may be. What's the deal?"

"One of my boys is going to ride in the horse race," Marcus said. "Loomis Depro."

Goodwin smirked a laugh. "Let me guess. You think he's good enough to beat Pendarrow."

"He might be. But he won't. He's going to lose the race."

"I see. So all we have to do is bet on Pendarrow, is that it?"

"That's it."

"Quinn, has it occurred to you that your man probably won't even have to lose the race on purpose? I believe Pendarrow can beat him anyway and so will everyone else. You probably won't be able to find anyone who will even bet on your man, and if you do find someone, the odds will be so great that you won't make any money."

"Maybe we can fix that," Quinn suggested.

"You got a way in mind?"

"I know the fella that takes care of Pendarrow's horse," Marcus said. "For one hundred dollars, he'll put somethin' in the horse's feed just before the race. That'll slow the horse down . . . not enough so's anyone will notice but enough to let Loomis win."

Goodwin looked shocked. "What? You think you can really do that?"

Marcas smiled.

"By God!" Goodwin said, slamming his right fist

into the palm of his left hand. "By God, with the odds .. . we'll bet on ..."

"Pendarrow, just like I said," Marcus interrupted. The smile left Goodwin's face, and he stared at Marcus and Hank as if he hadn't understood the word.

"Pendarrow? But if you're going to fix the race . . ."

"I said it would be a sure thing," Marcus said. "Doping the horse is not sure . . . telling Loomis to lose is. But, if we tell a few people... just a few, 'trusted' people ..."

"You don't have to go on, I know what you're saying!" Goodwin said. "We'll tell them Pendarrow's horse is going to be doped. They'll tell a few close friends, and they'll tell a few others, not only will we find people who will take our bets . . . we'll even be able to change the odds," Goodwin said. "I got to hand it to you, Quinn. That's a brilliant idea."

"Cover everyone's bets," Marcus said. "Put everything on Pendarrow."

"That might run as much as two or three thousand dollars," Goodwin said.

"The more you bet, the more you'll make. I want a thousand dollars for setting it up."

"You got it."

"I want it now," Marcus said. He smiled. "We're going to want to place a few bets ourselves." Goodwin walked over to the safe and twirled the dial for a moment, then took out a stack of greenbacks. He

ROBERT VAUGHAN

counted the money out and put a thousand dollars in Marcus's hands.

"Mr. Quinn," he said. "I think we've formed a most profitable relationship."

"Yeah," Marcus said. "That's just what I was thinkin'."

After they left the Land Commission office, Marcus and Hank walked back down the boardwalk toward the hotel. A large banner was strung across the street. It swung gently in the breeze, and the sign in front of Dr. Conkling's Apothecary, to which the banner was attached, made a squeaking sound as they walked by. The banner read: Ristine, Nevada wishes Happy Birthday to the U.S.A.

"Have you ever noticed that the greedier a sono-fabitch is, the easier it is to take their money?" Marcus asked.

Hank chuckled. "Yeah, and you know, I don't think I've ever enjoyed taking anyone's money as much as I'm gonna enjoy takin' his. Now, all Loomis has to do is win."

"Seems simple enough," Marcus said.

"Wonder where the boy is?"

"I don't know. I hope he's in the saddle; he needs a good workout."

At that very moment, Penny's fingers were digging into Loomis' back while she lay beneath him, mindless, in the throes of pleasure. She bucked beneath him as the spasms of release rippled through her flesh like wildfire. She arched her back, and Loomis felt her fingernails dig in deeper. Then she fell back as he bore deeper, pulling back and holding it in exquisite agony for a long moment before plunging back into the churning hot cauldron of her sex.

They settled into an even rhythm of lovemaking, and he kissed her small, hard breasts, making her squirm with delight. She held onto him and rocked with him, as if they were on the back of an easy-running horse. He stroked her gently, matching his movements to hers until shoots of pleasure coursed through his flesh, making him tingle all over.

Penny rushed to the edge of excitement, and she urged Loomis to take her to the height once more. He felt his seed boil and strain, and she sensed the urgency in him. Their strokes came faster and faster until he was no longer able to hold back, and he burst inside her, burst like a dam giving way, gushing into her like a spewing fountain.

"Oh," she gasped, holding him in her arms, locking her legs around him, pulling him into her until he was totally spent.

They lay in each other's arms for a long, quiet moment, listening to the sounds of each other's breathing, the soft whisper of the breeze against the windowpanes. Afternoon sunlight streamed through the curtains and dappled their naked bodies.

"Was it worth missing out on your afternoon nap?" Loomis asked.

"It was wonderful," Penny said. "I knew it would be ... I knew it would be better than any time has ever been before."

Loomis got out of bed and padded over to the chair where he had laid his clothes when he dropped in on her this afternoon. Penny stayed in bed, still naked, stretching languorously as she watched him through narrowed, green eyes. In this light and stretching in such a way as to diminish her curves, she looked more the little girl than the woman she had become.

"How'd you get that scar?" she asked, pointing to a long, ugly puff of discolored skin that started in the middle of his chest and worked its way down in a lightning streak to the right side of his thigh.

"Arkansas toothpick," Loomis answered.

"What's that?"

"A knife."

"You were in a knife fight?" she shuddered.

"Yeah, I was pretty young," Loomis said.

"Did the other man get hurt?"

"No," Loomis said, matter-of-factly. "He got kilt." Loomis pulled his pants on, then his shirt. He looked at her and smiled. "If you don't mind, maybe we'll do this again sometime."

Penny smiled. "I take my nap same time every day."

Some distance away, at the westernmost terminus of the railroad, a very small man, well-dressed and smoking an outsized cigar, stood on the depot platform and watched as a black groomsman walked a horse down from one of the train cars. At first the horse shied at stepping onto the ramp, but the groomsman spoke softly to it, holding the horse by its halter, and the animal started down.

"I say, Moses, do be careful with Dancer, or so help me, I shall have the skin stripped from your black hide," the small man said. His language was cultured, and he spoke with a distinct English accent.

"Yes, suh, Mr. Pendarrow. They ain't nothin' bad gonna happen to this here hoss long as I'm around. You hear that, Dancer? Moses gonna take real good care of you."

Dancer was a beautiful horse. His coat was a glistening chestnut in color, while his unusually long tail was almost blond. He was just under seventeen hands at the withers and completely blemish free. He tossed his head and raised his legs high as he moved down the ramp, calming down only when he was on solid ground. He nuzzled Moses, as if thanking him for leading him down.

A very pretty, dark-haired, dark-eyed woman walked over to stand beside Pendarrow. She was almost a head taller than he was.

"Look at Dancer nuzzle up to Moses," she said. "Sometimes I think that horse likes Moses more than he does you."

"Then the horse has misplaced loyalty." Pendarrow said. He looked at her critically. "The horse can be forgiven for that. He is a dumb animal. There is no excuse for your own, my dear."

"I'm not sure, but it sounds like you have just told me I am smarter than your horse. Perhaps I should thank you for the compliment."

"Smarter, perhaps," Pendarrow said. "But a possession just the same."

"And Moses? Is he a possession, too?"

"Of course."

"Perhaps the news didn't reach England, Jason. Slavery is outlawed now."

Pendarrow took his long cigar from his mouth and waved it. "Carol, my dear, the person who controls the purse strings will always be master to those who are dependent upon that purse."

Carol sighed. "You don't love me, Jason. Why do you insist on keeping me around?"

"You are a beautiful woman. Men who are more physically endowed, more handsome than I, covet you. Other men do make advances to you, do they not?"

"Yes."

"Of course they do. They want you, but only I can have you. That pleases me."

"What if I surprised you one day by accepting an offer? Your little game would go sour, wouldn't it?"

Pendarrow chuckled. "My dear, you only belittle yourself by making such empty threats. If you ever did find yourself wanting to stray, you would never have the courage to do so openly. You know who your master is, don't you?"

Carol turned away, but Pendarrow reached out and grabbed her by the arm. "I believe 1 asked you a question," Pendarrow said. "Do you, or do you not acknowledge me as your lord and master?"

Carol's face flushed red in anger. Finally, under his glare, she gave in. "I do," she said quietly.

Pendarrow smiled and stuck the cigar back in his mouth. "There, now, don't you feel better?"

"Yes," Carol mumbled.

"Mr. Pendarrow?" someone called, and the jockey looked up to see a man coming toward him from the depot. The man was smiling broadly, and he stuck his hand out. "Lindsey's the name. I'm the depot manager here. Let me tell you what a pleasure it is to have you stop in our little town. Yes, sir, you're a famous man, a very famous man. People all over the West have heard of you."

"I telegraphed ahead to hire a conveyance," Pendarrow said. "Have the necessary arrangements been made?"

Lindsey chuckled. "It's all ready. You know, I love to hear you English fellas talk." Lindsey looked at Carol. "This beautiful lady be your wife?"

"Yes," Pendarrow said.

"Pleased to meet you, ma'am," Lindsey said, shaking her hand vigorously. "You must be mighty proud of your husband, him bein' so famous an' all."

"Yes," Carol said in a flat, expressionless voice. "I'm very proud."

"Moses, kindly see to our luggage, then attach Dancer to the rear of the carriage," Pendarrow said.

"Yes, suh, Mr. Pendarrow," Moses answered.

Pendarrow turned to Carol. "I'm going down the street to the pub. You remain here."

"All right," Carol said. She turned to Lindsey. "Is there a place I can wash my face and hands?"

"Yes'm, they's a ladies' washroom in the depot there." Lindsey said.

"Thank you."

Lindsey waited until Pendarrow and Carol were both gone; then he walked toward Dancer. Moses was rubbing the animal down.

"Hey, you, Moses, that your name?"

Moses looked up, surprised that Lindsey would come over to talk to him.

"Yes, sir," he said. "Moses W. Moss."

"Did you get ever'thin' took care of?" Lindsey winked, conspiratorially.

"Took care of?"

"You know, with the horse. I aim to place me a bet on the race if you got the horse took care of."

"Yes, sir, I took care of everything," Moses answered. He wasn't sure what the man was talking about, but he learned long ago it was best to just agree with anything white people said.

"Damn!" Lindsey said, smiling broadly. "Damn, I

wasn't sure it was true. Now that I see it is, I'm gonna bet me a bundle."

"Yes, sir, I expec's you will," Moses said.

Lindsey hurried back to the depot. He walked over to the little window that opened into the Western Union office.

"Hackett," Lindsey called to the telegrapher. "I want you to send a message to Ristine. I just talked to the fella that's watchin' after Pendarrow's horse. Everythin' has been took care of."

Back in Ristine Lindsey's telegraphed message passed around the town like wildfire. From the old men who sat whittling on the corner of the porch in front of the dry goods store, to the checker players under the tree across from the bank, to the drinkers in the saloon, the word went out. Within an hour nearly everyone in town knew that Dancer's trainer had been bought off, and the fix was in. Everyone rushed to get their bets down, and Barlow Goodwin was covering them all.

Back in the Grand Hotel, Hank was reporting all the gambling activity to Marcus.

"From what I hear, Goodwin's already got five thousand dollars out coverin' the bets," Hank reported.

"Good.".

"Yeah, I guess so. Only thing is, what with all the heavy bettin' on either Loomis or Pendarrow, the other horses have dropped out."

"You mean there's not one other rider in this race?" Loomis asked.

"Just you and Pendarrow."

"I guess it's gonna come right down to it," Loomis said. "Me on one horse, Pendarrow on the other."

"Can you beat him?" Marcus asked.

"I got no problem with the rider," Loomis said. "It's his horse I'm worried about."

"You'll win," Hank said.

"Thanks for believin' in me, Hank."

"Yeah," Hank said, then he smiled broadly at Marcus.

"Before we put out this rumor 'bout dopin' the Pendarrow horse, they weren't more'n five people in this town thought Loomis had a chance in hell of winnin' that race . . . and them five was us, Seems to me like we could'a just bet real heavy with the odds on our side, and we could'a cleaned up."

"We could have. But then we wouldn't have Goodwin into it with every cent he has in town. When Loomis wins this race, most of the folks in town that's been cheated out of their money are going to have it back. That's 'cause they're all bettin' on Loomis, and Goodwin is covering every bet that's put down."

"That's true. And you can't believe who all is bettin'. Why, there's store clerks, cowhands, the schoolmarm, even the girls workin' here in the whorehouse. I just hope we're doin' the right thing."

"Do you think they would have bet on Loomis if they didn't believe they had an edge?"

Hank chuckled. "No, I reckon not. But I still gotta ask you, Marcus, what's in it for us? Why are we givin' these town folk their money back? We ain't in the business to give money back to fools who didn't have sense enough to hang on to it in the first place."

"We're not givin' the money back, Goodwin is," Marcus said. "And when he does that, he's gonna be all out of money. Only he can't run the business he's runnin' here without money, and lots of it. That means he's gonna need a fresh supply. Where do you think he's gonna get it?"

"From the railroad?" Hank asked.

"And how is it gonna get here?"

"Well, they'll probably send it on .. ." Hank stopped in midsentence, then smiled broadly. "Sonofabitch!" he said. "Sonofabitch! We're gonna rob us a train, ain't we?"

"Well, we have robbed a few in our time, haven't we?" Marcus answered. "Matter of fact, we got pretty good at it, as I recall. The only thing, we never knew whether the train would be carryin' twenty dollars or two thousand dollars. This one we can figure it's gonna be carryin' at least five thousand, maybe more."

"Yeah," Hank agreed. "And this time, it's all for us."

"I thought you might like that."

Suddenly, the smile left Hank's face. "Damn, Marcus, I just thought of somethin'!"

"What's that?"

"This whole thing depends on Loomis winnin' that race."

"That's right."

"You think maybe we better do somethin' to see to it that he does win?"

"You mean like dope Pendarrow's horse?"

"Well, that's what we've told ever'one we done."

"Yeah, and as many people as know now, don't you think it's going to get back to Pendarrow? He's gonna be watchin' that horse and his trainer every minute."

"What if. .." Hank started, then he stopped.

"What if what?"

"I was just thinkin'. If Goodwin gets a little nervous about puttin' out all this money, he might decide on his own to make certain that Loomis loses."

Marcus rubbed his chin for a moment as he thought about Hank's caution.

"You're right," he said. "We probably can't do anything about Pendarrow or his horse, but we can make sure that Loomis and his horse don't get some unwanted attention."

CHAPTER NINE

Barlow Goodwin was sitting at his desk studying a map. This wasn't the map he kept on the wall for the benefit of the townspeople and his commissioners, but a special map on which he plotted his progress in acquiring his own land. The map was marked with crosshatching and large squares, showing property that was now in his possession, and even the most casual glance indicated that he owned a substantial part of the land around Ristine. But there was still one large piece of land that he didn't own, a critical piece of land just inside Worthington Pass. The land in question was the five-thousand-acre tract that was being homesteaded by Miner Cobb.

Because of its location as the "front door of the valley", it was a choice piece of property. Ironically, the government had not provided the Kansas and Pacific with a grant to this land, because at that point, the railroad actually followed alongside the river at a point just beyond Cobb's ranch. Legally, Goodwin had no claim to the land. But that didn't stop him from wanting it . . . and he certainly didn't intend that it would stop him from getting it. He had tried to bluff Cobb off the land but without success. He had also tried to buy Cobb out and that had been equally unsuccessful. The last time he went out to the Cobb ranch with Fenton, he had practically been run off at the point of a gun.

Whatever it took to get the land, however, Goodwin would do, because once he had control of Cobb's land, he would own nearly all of Virgin River Valley. That meant he would also control the Virgin River . . . the only source of water for the entire valley. He had taken care of Luke McCabe, and McCabe had been every bit as stubborn as Cobb. He knew it would only be a matter of time until he had Cobb's land as well.

Goodwin had partners in his scheme to grab up all the land immediately adjacent to the railroad's route, but when he decided to broaden his ambition, to seek control of the entire valley, he began venturing out on his own. He had no partners in that operation, and he wanted none, for the fewer were involved, the larger the cut of the pie. Right now Goodwin was going after the whole pie, and ten years from now, with the Kansas and Pacific and Union and Pacific railroads providing transportation to the markets of the east and west and with every acre of fertile land and every drop of water under his control, he would be worth over one million dollars. The time had come to quit stalling and get the land.

"Mr. Fenton?"

The albino had been standing in the door of the office looking down the street. When Goodwin first hired Fenton, the albino used to make him nervous, spending so much time in the doorway staring down the street, rarely saying a word. But Goodwin learned that Fenton stayed inside because of his aversion to the sun, so he finally got used to it.

Fenton looked around fixing his pink-eyed stare on Goodwin.

"The time has come, Mr. Fenton," Goodwin said. He pointed to the map putting his finger on the only piece of land that wasn't crosshatched. "Cobb has been given every opportunity to leave. I want you to go out to his place and convince him to leave."

"I can have his woman?" Fenton hissed.

"Whatever it takes, Mr. Fenton," Goodwin replied.

Jeremy Cobb drank from the dipper, then poured the rest of the water over his head washing away the sweat from a hard day's work. When he reached for the towel he had draped across the split-rail fence, he found it was gone. He heard his sister laugh.

"Marcia," he said angrily. "Gimme the towel you took."

"What towel?" Marcia teased.

Jeremy rubbed the water out of his eyes, then opened them and saw the sixteen-year-old girl standing there holding the towel behind her back. She was smiling at him.

"If you don't want me to dry my face on your dress, you'll gimme that towel," Jeremy growled.

"Oh, you mean this towel?" Marcia said. She handed the towel to him.

"Thanks," Jeremy said. He took the towel and began drying his face.

"Are you going into town to the big bam dance and celebration on the Fourth of July?"

"I'm goin' in for the fireworks and the horse race," Jeremy said. "Don't care much for the dance."

"That's 'cause you're only fourteen," Marcia said. "When you get older ... as old as I am . .. you'll find out that's the best part of the whole celebration."

"Girls ain't nothing, always giggling and squirming around," Jeremy said. "I got more important things to do than spend time with some dumb girl."

"When all the girls you know turn into women, you won't feel like that."

"Oh, and I guess you're callin' yourself a woman now?"

"I'm sixteen."

Jeremy laughed. "You may be sixteen, but I know Papa won't let you go to the dance with Billy Cummings," he teased. "I heard you ask him, and I heard him tell you no. He said you were too young."

"Well, I'm going to meet him there, so what's the difference? Anyway, I'm not too young. Lots of women are married by the time they're sixteen."

"Maybe," Marcia answered.

"Who cares. What's for supper, anyway? I'm near 'bout starved."

"Breaded pork chops and fried potatoes," Marcia said. "And I made 'em myself."

"If you cooked it, we'll probably be poisoned," Jeremy teased.

As the brother and sister walked back up the path to the house, Marcia put her arm affectionately around

her younger brother, perhaps trying to show in that way that she was an adult now and old enough to be beyond any sibling squabbles. Jeremy pulled away from her, then ran up the path following the rich aroma of fried pork up to the house. He laughed, then waited for Marcia, pushing the door open just as she arrived. That's when both came to a complete halt, their eyes wide in shock. There, slumped forward on the table, was Miner Cobb. A pool of blood spread across the table from a cut on his throat.

"Papa!" Jeremy shouted, rushing to him. He lifted his head up and saw that his neck was covered with blood.

"Jeremy . .. look out!" Marcia shouted, but her warning was too late. Jeremy saw only the shadow of a movement, then something hit him on top of the head hard, and everything went black.

The man who hit Jeremy looked over at Marcia, and she felt her blood run cold. She knew who he was. He was the one with the mark of Satan on him, the white-haired man who had come with Mr. Goodwin to demand that her father sell the ranch. Why was he here? Marcia raised her hand to her mouth. She wanted to scream but she couldn't.

"Who is this girl?" Fenton hissed. "She the one stayed back in the house when we were here before?"

"Yes, that's my daughter," Marcia's mother said.

"I can see why you tried to hide her from me," Fenton said.

"No, I wasn't trying to hide her," Marcia's mother said. "I was just.. . that is . . . she is so young."

"Looks old enough to me," Fenton said, starting toward her.

"Please . .. please don't hurt her."

Marcia saw her mother then, saw that she was sitting in a chair with her arms pulled and tied behind her. Her mother's dress had been ripped down the front.

"Mama, what... what has he done to you?"

The albino smiled though the smile made him look even more evil.

"Well, now, I was about to take my pleasure from your mama, but I do believe I've changed my mind."

"Mama," Marcia whimpered, finally finding her voice again, "who is this man?"

"I killed your papa, girl. And I'll kill your mama and this boy if you don't do what I say."

"Please . . . please, don't kill them," Marcia said.

"You gonna be good to me then, girl? Real good?" He reached for her, but she twisted away from him, avoiding his grasp.

"Don't touch me! Go away! Please, just go away and leave us alone."

Fenton cocked his pistol and pointed it at Jeremy's head. "Girl, are you gonna be good to me, or do I pull the trigger, right now?"

"No, don't!"

"You're gonna be nice?"

Marcia nodded her head as tears slid down her cheeks.

The albino let the hammer down slowly. "I thought you might see it my way. You know what I want, don't you, girl?"

"I ... I think so," Marcia answered. She didn't know exactly, but she did have an idea.

"Good, then I don't have to waste time explainin'. Now, get outta that dress."

Marcia just stood there making no move to do what he said.

"Girl, if I have to tell you twice to do anything else, this boy's gonna die," Fenton hissed, and he pointed the pistol at Jeremy once again.

"Mama, is it gonna hurt?" Marcia asked in a weak, frightened voice.

"It... it won't be more than you can bear, child," her mother answered gently and started to cry.

After it was over, Marcia lay on the floor in her shame and pain as Fenton rebuttoned his pants. He nodded his head toward Jeremy.

"When the boy comes to, have him hitch up a team. Load up what you can carry, then get out of here. This land has been taken over by the Kansas and Pacific Railroad. If you're still here tomorrow, I'll come back."

"No!" Marcia's mother said quickly. "No, don't come back! We'll do what you say. We'll be gone."

It was near sunrise as Lucy Cobb poured the last of the coal oil on the front porch of the house, then she struck a lucifer, held it to a rag she had soaked in oil, and tossed it into the front room. As the fire caught, she looked through the flame and the smoke at her husband. It had been a struggle to lift him to the kitchen table, but she managed to get him there, then she dressed him in his Sunday suit. Next she folded his arms across his chest. In one hand she had put a lock of her hair, in the other a likeness of the family done last year when a traveling photographer had come through. Miner had set a great store by the likeness, often telling her that it would bring comfort to them in their old age.

Miner wouldn't be getting any older, and Lucy wanted him to have the likeness with him now. The flames began to lick at the legs of the table, and smoke curled up around his head. Lucy took a step back through the door.

"I'm sorry I couldn't bury you, Miner," she said quietly. "But I ain't gonna leave nothin' here for the railroad to have, not a house, and not a grave for them to desecrate. The Lord'll just have to understand that. Besides, I heard that they's some folks, even Christian folks, burns their dead. I reckon the Lord can find your spirit all the sooner iffen it's goin' up to him in the smoke."

Lucy left the little house that she had helped her husband build and walked quickly out to the wagon. Jeremy and Marcia were already on the wagon. Jeremy laid out in the back still sick from the bash on his head, Marcia sitting on the seat, staring straight ahead, as if unaware of what was going on.

Lucy wasn't too concerned about Jeremy's injury. She had seen ones like his before. A couple of years ago, Miner had been kicked in the head by a horse. Even when he came to, he was sick for a while. But he had gotten better in a few days.

No, it wasn't Jeremy she was worried about. It was Marcia. From the time that awful albino had left, Marcia hadn't spoken a word. She just sat there, staring out at the world, not even bothering to dress herself. Lucy had to dress her sixteen-year-old daughter as if she were a baby. But even that didn't bother her as much as the fact that Marcia wouldn't speak.

"Marcia, honey," Lucy said, climbing onto the seat

of the wagon and taking up the reins. "How are you feeling, girl?"

Marcia neither answered nor gave any indication that she had heard her mother speak.

"We're leaving this place," Lucy said. "We're going down to Flagstaff to live with my brother and his wife. Won't that be nice?"

Marcia didn't answer, and Lucy clucked at the team. The wagon pulled away while behind them the fire that had thus far been contained inside the house suddenly burst through the roof. Lucy could hear it now, a terrible roaring, popping sound. Miner was in there, and she blinked several times to keep the tears from coming down. She had done her weeping; now she had a family to look after.

"My brother and his wife's got 'em a real nice place down there," Lucy went on, acting as if she and Marcia were discussing the trip. "I think you and Jeremy will be real happy there."

One wall caved in, and even from this distance, Lucy could feel a blast of heat.

"Take a look at your brother, will you, dear? See if he's come to yet."

Marcia didn't move, so Lucy looked around at Jeremy. His eyes were closed, but Lucy could see that he was crying softly. She looked back at her daughter, so still and so quiet, and she shook her head.

CHAPTER TEN

NEARLY EVERYONE HAD HEARD OF JASON PENDARROW, and practically no one had heard of Loomis Depro. But the fact that so many people were willing to bet on Loomis made people curious, so by the evening of the third of July, the population of Ristine had grown by three times. All day long coaches and wagons had been coming from every town and ranch within fifty miles. Ristine filled, and men and women wandered up and down the boardwalks, spilled out into the street, and pitched camp under the big tree across from the bank unaware that it had recently been used to hang four men.

The merchants were already willing to declare the weekend a success, no matter how the race turned out, for many of the visitors to town took advantage to shop in the stores. They greeted all the visitors with friendly smiles, waving with one hand, while with the other they moved the price cards away from the merchandise to allow the demand to set the value of their goods and services.

The Grand Hotel was a scene of bustling activity. Every room was full, and men and women were crowded into the lobby. The noise level was so high that normal conversation was next to impossible. Everyone yelled at everyone else in order to be heard, and that only intensified the bedlam. Men waved drinks and cigars and even hands full of money as they tried to place last-minute wagers on the race that was to be held the next morning. Women, too, those who worked in the hotel and even a few of the more brazen ladies from the town and the visitors, were caught up in the excitement. They were no less vociferous than the men, so that occasionally a high-pitched shrill of laughter would ring out above everything else.

Though Jason Pendarrow was enjoying the acco-lades of all his well-wishers, Loomis was avoiding them. When Hank went looking for him, he found him out by the hotel stable leaning on the fence watching quietly as Moses prepared Dancer for the night. Moses had given the animal a workout earlier in the day, and if the horse was impressive while standing still, he was even more so in motion.

"Oh, here you are," Hank said. "I been lookin' for you."

Loomis glanced up, then smiled. He pointed toward Dancer. "Ever see a horse like that?" he asked.

"Can't say as I have."

"I ain't, either," Loomis said. Loomis ran his hand through his hair. "Hank, I don't mind tellin' you, we done bit off more'n we can chew."

"You don't think you can beat Pendarrow?"

"Only a fool could lose ridin' on the back of an animal like that. And I don't reckon Pendarrow's a fool."

"Maybe we really should doctor the horse."

"No!" Loomis said quickly. "I wouldn't want to see a horse like this messed with, even if you could get to him, which you can't. Anyhow, it wouldn't mean nothin' to me to win if I won knowin' the horse was fooled with."

"I thought you said they wasn't no way you could win," Hank said.

"That don't mean I'm gonna just stay at the starting line," Loomis replied. "I seen Pendarrow up on Dancer this afternoon. He's pretty good, but I think I'm better. I got a good horse . . . not as good as Dancer, but a good horse. Maybe me bein' a better rider is all it'll take."

"Maybe," Hank said. "Listen, I come out here to see if you wanted a drink."

"No," Loomis answered almost distractedly. "I think I'll just stay out here a while longer."

Hank put his hand on Loomis's shoulder, then returned to the hotel.

Pushing through the boisterous crowd, he went upstairs to his room. There, he checked on the figures he had been keeping. According to his calculations, the Raiders had five hundred dollars bet on the race at even odds. Most of the town of Ristine had bet on Loomis, though most of the visitors . . . either not aware that the "fix" was supposed to be in, or not believing it, had bet on Pendarrow. Their influx of money had kept the odds even. The most important entry among his figures was the note that Barlow Goodwin had covered every bet and was now without cash.

All their plans centered around Goodwin losing the bet and having to send back for more cash. Now, after his brief conversation with Loomis, Hank was worried that Loomis would lose and the plan would fall through.

The boys had done nothing to interfere with Pendarrow's horse. Marcus said it was too risky, while Loomis was insistent that nothing be done that could harm the horse.

"It ain't the money. Hell, after the race we can steal the goddamn money back. But the race is gonna be fair."

Hank knew that was Loomis's pride talking. But from what Loomis told him out by the stable, pride wasn't going to be enough to win this race. He decided he'd better find Marcus. Maybe Marcus could come up with an idea.

Hank left the room and closed the door quietly behind him. When he stepped out of the room, he saw a woman standing at the window at the back end of the hall. She was tall and willowy with long black hair. From this angle and in the dim light of the hall, Hank couldn't see her face. He could tell though that she was certainly put together well.

Hank cleared his throat, and the woman looked around quickly.

"Beg pardon, ma'am," Hank said, tipping his hat. "Didn't mean to startle you none."

The woman smiled broadly, and the smile literally lit up her face. She took a couple of steps into the light, allowing him to see her more clearly. Her face was oval, the nose straight and thin, the mouth full with painted lips that were wet and slightly puckered. From here he could smell a faint perfume like crushed flowers.

"You didn't startle me, Mr. Proudy."

Hank was surprised. He had not seen her before, and he was sure she wasn't one of the girls who worked for Maggie.

"You know who I am?"

The woman laughed a rich, deep-throated chuckle. "Ah, I do believe that gives me the advantage," she said. She walked up to him and stuck out her hand. When he took it, he felt skin that was soft, cool, and smooth. "You're one of the friends of the jockey who will be riding against my husband."

"You're Mrs. Pendarrow?"

The woman came closer. "You can call me Carol."

She was close enough now that Hank could look into her nut-brown eyes. He saw the stars dance and sparkle like cut diamonds.

"My pleasure, Carol," Hank said quietly, almost intimately.

"Tell me," Carol said with a faint curl to her mouth, a bemused smile. "Why are you betting against my husband? He always wins."

"Begging your pardon, ma'am, but no man always wins."

Carol laughed aloud. "You don't know my husband."

Hank stroked his chin as he studied Pendarrow's wife.

"Why do I feel like you wouldn't be particularly unhappy if Mr. Pendarrow loses this race?"

"I would like nothing better than to see that arrogant little bastard I'm married to lose," she said.

Hank smiled. "Well, ma'am, let's hope Loomis doesn't disappoint you.'"

Carol smiled and turned in such a way as to thrust her hip out, drawing her dress so tight against her flesh that Hank could see the outline of her pelvic bone beneath the cloth. His blood turned hot and began flowing to his loins.

"Now, tell me, Mr. Proudy, do you have anything you must do right now? Any last-minute bets you must put down or anything like that?"

"No, nothing."

He smile grew more sultry. "Then, if you wanted to,

you could show me your room, couldn't you?" She stepped boldly up to him and put her arms around his neck pressing her full breasts into his chest. Her thighs pressed against his own, and her perfume overwhelmed him. As she rubbed against him, he was reminded of a cat rubbing against a person's ankle, begging for affection.

"Showin' you my room would be a good idea at that," Hank said in a husky voice. "Because if we don't get somewhere soon, I'm gonna put you down right here on the hall floor."

She shivered, moving still closer to him. His manhood swelled and throbbed under his trousers, and he felt her rub herself against it. The swelling intensified.

"Here on the hall floor or in your room," she said. "It doesn't matter. All I know is that I want you."

Hank tilted her head up toward his and kissed her on the lips. They were still standing in the hall and could be discovered at anytime by anyone, including her husband. But that didn't matter to Hank, and it didn't seem to matter to Carol for she responded to his kiss with a willingness that was sudden and fiery. Her mouth was as sweet as crushed mint leaves, and he probed it with his tongue, feeling her surge against him with even more urgency. Her loins rubbed up and down his hard shaft pressing her sex against it.

Finally she broke off the kiss and smiled up at him. "I meant it when I said you could take me on the hallway floor," she said. "But we might find it more comfortable in your bed."

Hank took her back to his room, opened the door, then pulled her inside. As he closed the door with one hand, he began unbuttoning the back of her dress with the other, loosening the loops, slipping them free. She was kissing him again with kisses that were wet and hungry. Now it was time for her tongue to explore his mouth, and he felt it flit about like a serpent, probing here and there with its hot pleasure.

The dress fell to the floor, and Hank stepped back to look at her. She was in a chemise now, her legs bare below her knees. She made no effort to cover herself, but slipped out of her undergarments, then stood before him naked and beautiful.

"Hurry," she urged.

A moment later, with Hank standing nude before her, she reached out and touched his hard, throbbing penis. She squeezed it gently, her fingers wrapping around it, while he touched her breasts, rubbing his fingers lightly across the tips of her nipples. She winced with a sudden shiver, and he scooped her up and carried her to bed.

Hank crawled into bed with her, and as they embraced, his penis stiffened with a fresh rush of blood through the veins. Carol grabbed him as Hank began stroking the clefted lips of her sex, probing past the velvety inner lining until she gasped. Her hand moved up and down his shaft, teasing it with a desperation born of passion.

Hank could wait no longer then, and he rolled over on her. She raised her legs and pulled him closer. He shoved himself deep into her. She wrapped her legs around him and squeezed him between her thighs, while with her long fingernails, she scratched at his back. She rocked in rhythmic counterpoint to his thrustings, her back arching like a stretching cat. Hank felt as if his penis had been submerged in a vat of hot oil. Pleasure rushed through him, and he drove hard with deep strokes, letting the good feeling rise up in him, pumping faster and faster into her honeyed sheath.

Carol whimpered in pure pleasure as he jetted his seed into her. Her fingers continued to dig into his back, and she hung onto him as if afraid to let go. Finally, emptied, spent, and sated, Hank fell atop her. He saw the rosy pallor in her cheeks, on her neck, and he kissed her gently.

"And to think," Carol said, "that I didn't want to come to Ristine."

Hank got up from the bed. She lifted her arms and put her hands behind her head causing her breasts to disappear, to be marked only by her erect nipples. She looked up at him, a soft smile curling her lips.

"I can give you an edge," she said.

"What?"

"You can't do anything to the horse, because Moses,

the stablehand, won't let you. But I can give you an edge in the race that will help your man beat Jason."

Hank looked hard into her eyes. "You hate him that much?"

"Uhmm," she said, sighing in contentment. "Let's just say you've earned the favor."

"Don't think I don't appreciate your offer," he said. "But Loomis is a proud little shit. He wouldn't ride if he thought there was any cheatin' goin' on. We talked about it."

"He wouldn't even have to know anything about it. Besides, this isn't cheating," Carol said. She sat up, and her breasts, which had been flattened by her supine position, now fleshed into place full and round.

"I'm listening," Hank said as he packed his shirt tail into his pants.

CHAPTER ELEVEN

LOOMIS HAD SLEPT FITFULLY THAT NIGHT. OUTSIDE HIS room, men and women had hurried up and down the hallways all night long, shouting to each other, laughing, in general being boisterous. Several times during the night, he had heard Penny's voice as she took customer after customer into her room, and once he heard a couple of the other girls talking about how much money they had made in the last twenty-four hours.

The result of so little sleep was greeting the morning more tired than he had been when he went to bed the night before. Despite this, he was glad to see the new day arrive, because this was the day of the race ... the day it would all be over, one way or another. So, as soon as it was full light, he was up and dressed and down to the stable to see to his horse.

When Loomis stepped out into the gray light of

morning, he saw Moses standing in the mist, tending to Dancer.

"Mornin' Mr. Loomis," Moses said,

"Good morning, Moses."

"Mr. Loomis, I hopes you don' mind," Moses said. "But this momin' when I feed Dancer, I give some of it to your hoss, too."

Loomis chuckled. "Did my horse tell he wasn't gonna get to eat?"

Moses laughed with him. "No, suh, nothin' like that," he said. He patted Dancer on the neck. "But Mr. Jason, he gets some kind'a special feed sent to him from Kentucky. It's a blend of oats, cornmeal, molasses, an' alfalfa. Mr. Jason, he swears by it, says it's the best thing they is for a hoss to eat on the day it's gonna race."

"Why, I thank you, Moses," Loomis said. He studied the old black man for a moment. Though he was from Mississippi, his family had never been wealthy enough to own slaves. Nevertheless, he had been around black people a lot, and he knew that they were sometimes moved to do something just because they felt that it was right. "The question is, why'd you do it?"

"You seems like a man what has a love for hosses, Mr. Loomis. I seen the way you been lookin' at Dancer."

"He's a damn fine horse."

Moses smiled. "Dancer, he see a hoss tryin' to pass him, he just naturally got to give his entire heart to hold 'em off. And, Mr. Loomis, he's got more heart than any hoss I ever been aroun'."

Loomis sighed. "Yeah, I sort of figured that. Well, if my critter's finished eatin', I reckon I'll give him a little mornin' exercise."

"Mr. Loomis?" Moses called to him as he started for the barn. Loomis turned to look back at him. "Maybe they's one thing you should know. I give this hoss his name, Dancer. You know why I done that?"

"No."

"'Cause he's got a natural stridin' rhythm, Mr. Loomis. That's why he run so fast. Only thing is, if somethin' was to happen that would cause him to lose his rhythm right in the middle of his runnin', it would, like as not, take four or five seconds for him to get it back. You see, he's got his own beat, here," Moses put his hand over Dancer's heart. "It don't come from Mr. Jason. Only Mr. Jason, he don't know that, and if somethin' happen'd why he'd be tryin' to get Dancer to runnin' with *his* rhythm 'stead of his natural one. You understand what I'm talkin' about?"

"Yes," Loomis said. "If Dancer would happen to break stride, I've got a chance."

"Yes, suh," Moses said.

"You ever see Dancer break stride before?"

"Yes, sir, two times. That's how come I know about it. Thing is, it didn't make no difference either time. Dancer, he's so fast, he come back and beat the other hosses both times. I expec's if that happens in this race, Dancer will still win."

"I reckon," Loomis said. Armed with this piece of information, he had a chance against Pendarrow. "Moses?"

"Yes, suh?"

"Thanks."

Moses smiled broadly. "That's all right, suh. Good luck."

Race time was at 10:00 A.M. Though only two horses were in the race now, that had the effect of making the race even more exciting for the spectators. It would be one to one, one horse and rider against the other. This way there would be no divided loyalties. Everyone in the crowd had placed their money on one rider or the other, so they would cheer as one when the horses came back across the finish line.

By 9:30 the sidewalks on both sides of Main Street were crowded with people. A handful of boys held an impromptu footrace down the middle of the street, and their efforts brought cheers from the crowd now in a very festive mood. Firecrackers were popping every minute or so, and a few of the more intoxicated celebrants, dissatisfied with the modest popping of a firecracker, would fire their pistols in the air. Whenever that happened, one of the commissioners would quickly make an arrest, showing the town that they were there, not just to carry out Barlow Goodwin's orders, but to see to the public order.

A hasty observation tower had been built in front of the Land Commission office, and one of the men of the town, an auctioneer equipped with field glasses, had climbed to the top. From there he would be able to call down reports to the others as to the progress of the race. The racecourse started at a chalk line poured across the street in front of the Land Commission office, proceeded all the way down the length of the street, past the Grand Hotel, and onto a point about half a mile beyond the edge of town. There, the course circled a large cottonwood tree, then came back over the same route by the Grand Hotel again, and down the street to the finish line.

A few last-minute wagers were still being placed, though most of the betting had already been accomplished. G.B. Greer was wandering up and down the street interviewing visitors to Ristine, putting together notes for what would be his special, Independence Day edition to come out later that day.

Back at the hotel stable, Marcus, Bob, and Billy Joe were with Loomis. Billy Joe had cut down a saddle so that it weighed less than half what an ordinary saddle would weigh, and he was making a few last-minute adjustments to it as Bob saddled the horse.

"Loomis, how the hell can you hope to win if this horse don't even have a name?" Bob asked. It had been a running issue between the two brothers ever since they stole the horse from a ranch in southern Arizona.

"A name ain't gonna make him run no faster," Loomis said.

"Well, Loomis," Marcus said, patting the horse on the neck. "This here horse without a name got a chance?"

"Damn right he does," Loomis said. "I wouldn't even go out there if I thought I was gonna be made a fool of. He's a good horse."

"Wonder where Hank is?" Billy Joe asked.

"If I know Hank, he's found him a willin' woman somewhere," Loomis laughed.

"Yeah, but he ought to be here."

"Billy Joe, it don't bother me none if he ain't here," Loomis said. "Hell, if he was ridin' this race and I had a woman willin' to be bedded, that's where I'd be."

Bob laughed. "If Hank was ridin' this race, bein' with a woman would be the best thing, 'cause he wouldn't have the chance of a snowball in hell."

"Billy Joe, you got that saddle about ready?" Marcus asked.

"Yep."

"All right. You get over by the bank. Bob, you get down by the boot store. I'll be down by the hotel. Ever'body keep your eyes open."

"Yeah," Loomis said. "I sure don't want any surprises happenin'."

"Little brother, you just ride like hell," Bob said. "They ain't gonna be no surprises, I promise you that."

"Well," Loomis said, swinging up into the saddle, "it's time to get to it."

As Loomis rode down the street toward the starting line, there were several who applauded him. They were letting him know that they didn't expect to be let down.

Goodwin was standing near the starting line with Tanner and Gilmore. He watched Loomis ride down the street toward him, and suddenly something inside told him that Loomis Depro had no intention of throwing this race. He couldn't explain it. . . . Perhaps it was the arrogant way he sat on his horse, or the way his eyes took in the crowd. Whatever gave him the notion, he couldn't deny it. Despite what Marcus Quinn had promised.

"Tanner," Goodwin said. When the commissioners looked around, Goodwin pointed to the boot store. "You get down there behind the boot store. If Depro has the lead then . . . take care of it." Tanner nodded and took off.

"Gilmore, you get down there by the hotel. We don't want our partners pulling a double cross on us."

"I'll take care of it," Gilmore promised.

"Ladies and gentlemen!" the announcer in the tower shouted through his megaphone. "This here rider approachin' us now is Loomis Depro. Move back and give him room."

Loomis rode the full length of the street looking on both sides at the faces of the hundreds who had gathered in town for the race. He saw Penny, and she blew him a kiss. He smiled and raised his hand toward her in a wave. A couple of kids darted out from the crowd, then ran along beside him as he rode toward the starting line.

"You gonna win the race, mister?"

"I'm gonna try."

"You ain't gonna do it. I done seen the other horse."

"Yeah," Loomis said with a small smile. "I seen 'im, too."

"And now, ladies and gentlemen, Mr. Jason Pendarrow!" the announcer shouted through the megaphone.

The crowd applauded again, and mixed with the applause, Loomis heard several exclamations of surprise. When he turned his horse around, he saw the reason for their reaction. Jason Pendarrow was wearing knee-length, highly polished black leather boots, white silk pants, and a cherry red silk shirt. On his head was a small, red cap. A bright red silk was under his tiny saddle, while a red mask, with holes cut for his eyes, was around Dancer's head. Though Pendarrow was sitting in the saddle, the horse was being led by Moses, who was wearing an outfit of the same colors. When they reached the starting line, Moses turned the horse around and handed the reins up to Pendarrow. The jockey took them, then leaned toward Loomis.

"I'm told there are more than a few of these people who have been foolish enough to place wagers on your winning."

"That's what I hear."

"Something about Dancer being doctored, I believe."

"Just a rumor."

"Yes, and not a very good one. Sometimes, Depro, I hold back a little so the chap from the hometown isn't too badly embarrassed by the thrashing I give him. This time, however, I shall enjoy making you look the fool that you are."

"I wouldn't want it no other way," Loomis answered.

Barlow Goodwin was the starter. He looked down the street, satisfied himself that Tanner and Gilmore were in position in case they were needed, then he stepped to one side of the starting line and raised his pistol.

"Gentlemen, are both of you ready?" he asked.

"Quite ready, thank you," Pendarrow answered.

"I reckon I am," Loomis said. He held the reins loosely in his hands and poised himself, feeling every muscle in his horse tense in readiness. He had raced this horse enough times now that the animal knew exactly what was expected of him, and Loomis knew it would give him all it had. The only question, of course, was would it be enough.

"When I shoot my gun, go," Goodwin said.

Loomis sat quietly for a moment waiting for the starter's pistol. During this brief moment, he pictured in his mind the finish line, with him crossing it first.

The gun fired, and the crowd roared. Pendarrow used his whip from the very start. Dancer shot forward like a bullet, and Pendarrow immediately steered Dancer in front of Loomis. He was a full length ahead of Loomis as they passed the boot shop, two lengths by the time they reached the Grand Hotel on their way out of town. Then, at the quarter mile mark just beyond the edge of town, Loomis's horse started to move up with long, steady strides.

Dancer was a fine, noble horse, and when he saw Loomis closing on him, his competitive spirit came into play; and he reopened up a lead of one length. Loomis's horse hung in, so though Dancer got a length lead, he couldn't stretch it out any further.

They reached the cottonwood tree, then swung around it and started back toward town.

"They're startin' back!" the announcer called. He was looking through binoculars toward the distant tree.

"Who's in front?"

"Pendarrow!"

Several people cheered, others groaned.

"But Depro is staying close!"

Loomis knew that his horse was giving him all he had, knew that he was running above himself because he was being pulled along by the speed of Dancer. If so much weren't riding on this race he could enjoy it for the sheer fun of it. But he needed to win. More than that, he wanted to win, to show up the arrogant little bastard in front of him.

As they approached the Grand Hotel on the way back into town, they saw someone on the upstairs balcony looking out toward the cottonwood tree.

"What the hell?" Loomis said aloud. There, on the balcony, he saw a beautiful, naked woman waving and smiling at them.

"Hello, Jason!" the woman yelled. At that moment Loomis saw Hank step through the window from behind the woman. Like her, he was naked. With a smile, the woman sank to her knees in front of Hank and took him in her mouth.

"Carol!" Pendarrow shouted in one long, agonizing scream.

Pendarrow jerked awkwardly on his horse, and Dancer's stride was broken. In those few seconds, Loomis could take the lead, and this close to the finish line, he might be able to hold on to it!

Back at the tower by the starting line, the announcer had seen Dancer falter, and Loomis close in, though of course, as Hank and Carol were on the other side of the hotel, no one knew what had caused the slight falter.

"Depro is chargin' Pendarrow!" the announcer shouted. "He's chargin' hard! Now he's passed him! Depro has the lead! Depro has the lead!"

Those who had bet money on Loomis roared loudly. Goodwin looked down the street, caught Gilmore's attention, then nodded. Gilmore stepped behind the building, then raised his pistol.

"Drop it," Marcus said from behind Gilmore's back.

Gilmore dropped his pistol, then raised his hands.

"Don't shoot!" he called out in panic. "I wasn't gonna do nothin'."

"I didn't think so," Marcus said. "Get on out of here."

By that time the two riders thundered by the hotel, Loomis in the lead, but Dancer closing fast.

At the boot store, Tanner had no idea why Gilmore let Depro get by, but he didn't intend to. He raised his rifle, rested it on the top of a fence post, and took aim. Suddenly a huge arm came out from the corner of the building, snatched the rifle out of his hands, then smashed it into two pieces on the fence post.

"What the . . .?" Tanner shouted, but that was as far as he got, because Billy Joe's big fist slammed into his face, and Tanner went down..

The horses were one hundred yards from the finish line now, both riders bent low over their mounts, both raised up from their saddles holding themselves on with their knees. The horses' manes were flying, their nostrils distended, and their hooves drumming a thunder in the street. Dancer had closed to within half-length, a neck, a head... but when they crossed the finish line, Loomis won by a nose.

. . .

Those who had bet on Loomis rushed into the street to surround him, shouting their congratulations, laughing and screaming with the pleasure of having won so much money. Loomis looked around at Pendarrow who was sitting on his horse, twisted around in his saddle, glaring back toward the hotel.

CHAPTER TWELVE

JEREMY COBB HAD FORGOTTEN ALL ABOUT THE BIG RACE, and the Independence Day celebration. In fact, he'd forgotten it was the Fourth of July. He knew only that his father was dead and his sister might as well be—all because of one man.

The boy had left his mother and sister sleeping in their wagon at dawn and unharnessed Smoke, one of their horses. Taking his father's old Sharps .52-caliber rifle, he headed back to Ristine determined to find Fenton and kill him.

When he came into town, he saw more people than he'd ever seen at one time crowding around a tower that had been built at the far end of the street.

Puzzled, Jeremy slid off his horse, pulling his rifle down with him. He tied Smoke to a hitching rail, searching the crowd for the albino.

"Where at's your saddle, boy?" someone called to

Jeremy, and the heckler and the others with him laughed.

"I don't need one," Jeremy said, making an excuse for the fact that he didn't have one. "Mister, can you tell me what's a'goin' on here? Why's there so many people in town?"

"Why, you mean you wasn't here for the big horse race?"

Jeremy shook his head.

"You missed a good one, boy. That there English feller that ever'one says couldn't be beat, got hisself beat."

"I'm lookin' for someone," Jeremy said. Talk of the horse race didn't interest him. He had a mission to perform. He put his hand in front of his face. "He's real white all over. His face, his hair ..."

"The albino."

"The what?"

"That's what they call a feller that's white like that... albino. His name's Fenton. He's the chief commissioner."

"That's the one. You know where he's at?"

"He don't stay out in the sun much. Last I seen of him, he was standin' inside the Land Commission office down there just lookin' out at the goin's on."

"Where at's the Land Commission office?"

"Boy, don't you know nothin'? That's it down there, that place that's half buildin', half tent."

"Obliged," Jeremy said. Jeremy opened the breech of

the rifle and slipped a .52-caliber cartridge into the chamber. He closed the breech but left the hammer down so that the rifle wasn't cocked, then started down the middle of the street toward the Land Commission office.

All around him, people were shouting, laughing, singing, drinking, enjoying the celebration, and for many, the money they had just won as a result of betting on Loomis in the race. None of them seemed to pay any attention to the boy who was walking with measured pace and determined gaze toward the Land Commission office at the far end of the street. And he paid no attention to them.

Marcus was in the Land Commission office talking with Goodwin. Goodwin was furious.

"You jerked a cinch into me!" Goodwin said. "I thought we had a deal. I was to cover all the bets, and you was to make sure your man lost. I trusted you."

"Did you now?" Marcus replied. "Is that why you had two of your men out, set to ambush Loomis?"

"They were just there to make sure he carried out his end of the bargain," Goodwin said.

"Yeah and shoot him down if he didn't," Marcus replied.

"I can see now that..."

That was as far as Goodwin got, for at that moment, a large-caliber bullet buzzed through the office like an angry bee, slamming into the wooden part of the wall just behind Goodwin. That was followed almost immediately by the booming sound of a gun. It wasn't a pistol, and it wasn't a Henry carbine. It was a sound Marcus recognized at once, because it was a sound he had heard thousands of times during the war. It was the sound made by the firing of a breech-loading Sharps. "What the hell?" Goodwin yelled in fright.

"It's the Cobb boy," Fenton said from the doorway. "I should've killed him when I had the chance.

Fenton darted outside with Marcus heading out just behind him.

Standing in the middle of the street with the breech of his rifle open, Jeremy Cobb was reaching into his pocket for another shell.

Fenton fired while Jeremy was trying to reload, and he hit the boy in the arm. The rifle fell into the dirt. Fenton raised his pistol and took slow and deliberate aim.

"Say your prayers, boy," he hissed.

"Did you give my pa a chance to say his prayers?" Jeremy challenged defiantly. His rifle was in the dirt but hate was still in his eyes.

"Fenton," Marcus barked. "The boy's unarmed."

"Stay out of this, Quinn," Fenton replied.

"I ain't plannin' on just lettin' you shoot him down," Marcus said again.

Without saying another word, Fenton whirled toward Marcus and fired. Marcus felt the top of his ear sting as the bullet clipped off a tiny piece of flesh before it tore through the brim of his hat. Marcus pulled his gun and fired back even as Fenton was shooting a second time. Fenton's second bullet hit one of the posts that supported the observation tower, while Marcus's bullet plunged into Fenton's neck.

Fenton dropped his gun and grabbed his throat. The blood looked an exceptionally bright red against his maggot-white skin. He fell to his knees and gurgled, his pink eyes darting about open wide with terror.

"No!" Jeremy shouted. "Don't die, you sonofabitch, 'til I kill you!"

Jeremy grabbed Fenton's pistol up from the dirt where it had been dropped. He pulled the hammer back and shoved the end of the barrel into Fenton's face.

"Somebody stop that boy!" a man in the crowd shouted.

"Leave him be!" Marcus ordered, and the crowd, who had formed themselves into a semicircle around the bizzare event, held their breath and watched in morbid curiosity as the drama played itself out before them.

"Stay alive, mister," Jeremy pleaded, and now people could see the anger in his heart. "I want you to stay alive long enough to know that you was killed by the son of the man you murdered and the brother of the girl you raped."

Fenton made an effort to say something, but when he tried to speak, blood gushed from his mouth. His eyes darted across the crowd desperately as if seeking help from someone. He reached a blood-covered hand out toward Jeremy, the fingers curling and clawing at the air. He inched forward on his knees trying to get to the boy.

"Do you remember me?" Jeremy asked.

Fenton nodded his head yes, then his eyes drooped. Marcus saw the life beginning to leave them.

"Boy, if you're serious about doin' this, do it now."

Jeremy held the pistol in a solid grip, then he squeezed the trigger. The hammer came forward, and the gun boomed in his hand. The bullet hit Fenton in the forehead, then burst through the back of his head taking brain, blood, and bone with it. The impact of the bullet knocked Fenton back, and he lay in the dirt and his own gore, his pink eyes wide open.

Jeremy stared down at him for a moment longer; then he dropped the pistol in the dirt. He looked over at Marcus.

"I reckon I owe you my thanks, mister," he said.

"Who are you, boy?"

"My name's Jeremy Cobb."

"This man do all those things you said he did?" Marcus asked.

"Yes, sir. He come out to the ranch and said our land didn't belong to us no more. He was lyin'. My pa was workin' that land before I was borned; it didn't belong to the Kansas and Pacific Railroad. Pa wouldn't leave, so he killed him, raped my sister, then told my ma we had to go. Ma didn't even have time to bury pa. . .. She just put him in the cabin and set fire to it."

"What would the K. and P. want with your ranch?" someone asked. "I know where it is.... It ain't nowhere near where the railroad track is gonna be."

"I don't know nothin' about that," Jeremy said. "All I know is what this here man done."

"How about it, Goodwin?" G.B. Greer asked, pushing his way forward. "Did you send Fenton out to the Cobb ranch to do all that?"

"Of course not!" Goodwin shouted, pulling a silk handkerchief from his pocket and wiping the sweat away from his face. "If Fenton did all that, he was acting on his own. And far as I'm concerned, he should'a been killed."

"Where's your ma and sister now?" Marcus asked. He looked at the wound in the boy's arm, saw that the bullet had cut a groove but hadn't gone in. The boy was wearing a bandana around his neck, and Marcus used it to make a hasty bandage.

"They're out on the trail," Jeremy said, wincing once lightly as Marcus tightened the bandage into place. "I snuck away this mornin'."

"You can't go back to them, you know," Marcus said. "Not after this. It'll never be the same again."

"I ... I reckon not."

Marcus knelt down to run his hands through Fenton's pockets. He pulled out a bag of gold pieces. He threw one piece down on Fenton's still form.

"That's enough to bury him," he said. "You'll need the rest of it to get a fresh start somewhere else. That ain't gonna be none too easy for a kid."

"I'll make it," Jeremy said, stuffing the money in his pocket.

"I'm bettin' on it," Marcus said.

Jeremy reached down and picked up his rifle, then started back down the street to where he had left his horse. Like Moses parting the Red Sea, the people who had gathered around moved back to let him pass, then closed in again behind him.

Jeremy didn't say another word to anyone. When he reached his horse he swung onto the animal's back and headed him out of town. Only then did he let himself cry.

Back at the hotel, having missed the episode between Jeremy and Fenton, Loomis was out in the stable rubbing down his horse. Moses was in the next stall taking care of Dancer.

"You rode a good race, Mr. Loomis," Moses said.

"Did you see it?"

"Yes, suh, I was up here in the hayloft. I could see everything real good."

Loomis looked up at the hayloft, then checked the angle from the loft to the corner of the hotel. It wouldn't have been possible for Moses to have seen the scene played out between Pendarrow's wife and Hank on the other side of the hotel.

"I want to thank you, Moses, for tellin' me about Dancer an' his rhythm."

"Yes, suh," Moses said, continuing to rub down the horse. "But the truth is, I don't reckon I would'a told you if I'd known it was really gonna make Dancer lose the race. It near broke my heart to see him tryin' so hard at the end."

"Dancer didn't lose the race, Moses. Pendarrow did," Loomis said. "And if it had been another ten yards, Dancer would have caught me."

Moses smiled broadly. "Yes, suh, I expec's he would have. He is some game hoss, ain't he?"

"The best I ever seen."

"Wonder what it was made him lose his rhythm like that? From where I was standin' it looked like Mr. Jason jerk back on him for just a second."

"I don't reckon we can know what's goin' on in a man's head," Loomis said.

"No, suh, I guess not." Moses said. "I expec's we'll be leavin' this here place today. Mr. Jason, he got another race back in Denver."

"Moses, I hope Dancer wins that one, I truly do."

"Yes, suh," Moses said. The black man looked up at Loomis, then flashed him a big smile. "I expec's he'll have Miz Carol watchin' that one from the finish line. That ought to help some."

Loomis was surprised by Moses' comment, then he laughed out loud. So Moses did know what happened after all.

"You're a good man, Moses," Loomis said. "Too good a man to stay with that little sonofabitch."

"You want to buy this hoss, Mr. Loomis?"

Loomis looked at Dancer for a long moment. Owning a horse like that would be the dream of a lifetime, but it wasn't something that would would fit in with the way he lived. Dancer was bred for speed, not stamina, and though he was the fastest and most beautiful horse Loomis had ever seen, he wouldn't last two months with them.

"He's a good horse, but I reckon I won't be buyin' him," Loomis said.

Moses went back to rubbing the animal down, working his brushes over Dancer's skin briskly.

"Then I don't expec's I'll be leavin' Mr. Jason," Moses said.

Loomis finished with his horse, and he put the brush up, waved good-bye to Moses, then went to the hotel. Hank and Bob were waiting in his room.

"I was talking with Hank about the race," Bob said.

"No he wasn't," Hank interrupted. "He was gettin' on me for not watchin' it."

"Is that right?" Loomis asked, smiling broadly.

"Well, yeah," Bob said. "Seems to me like, with so much ridin' on this race an' all, Hank could'a at least watched it. 'Sides, me an' Billy Joe had to take care of those no 'count commissioners.'

"Hank saw it," Loomis said, smiling.

"Yeah? Where from?"

"The upstairs balcony, Pendarrow's room," Hank said.

Bob looked puzzled.

"You seen Pendarrow's wife?" Loomis asked.

"Yeah, pretty woman," Bob said. He stopped and looked at Hank. "Why, you sonofa—"

"You ever know Hank *not* to comfort a lonely wife?" Loomis asked.

They all laughed.

Hank had been stretched out on the bed; now he stood up. "If you boys will excuse me, I got a little gamblin' money in my pocket, an' there's folks visitin' in this town I ain't fleeced yet. I'm gonna find me a card game."

The Pendarrows left late on the afternoon of the Fourth and most of the visitors to town left the next day. It was two days later, on Monday, with the town of Ristine back to normal, when Goodwin sent the telegram message that Marcus was waiting for.

Marcus had come up with a plan. He knew that the telegrapher was one of the Grand Hotel's most frequent visitors, so he arranged with Helga for him to get one free night if he would bring to her any message sent by or delivered to Barlow Goodwin. As he knew he would, the telegrapher accepted immediately.

Marcus was sitting in the kitchen drinking coffee with Billy Joe when Helga brought the message to him.

"The telegrapher, this message he bring," she said.

"It was by Barlow, sent." She handed a yellow sheet of paper to Marcus.

Marcus read the message, printed in big, bold letters on the page.

KANSAS AND PACIFIC RAILROAD VIRGIN VALLEY LAND DEVELOPMENT ASSOCIATION DENVER COLORADO

HAVE RUN INTO SOME TROUBLE HERE STOP MUST HAVE FIVE THOUSAND DOLLARS IN NEGOTIABLE BILLS AT ONCE STOP FENTON IS DEAD STOP LOCAL COMMISSIONERS ARE NOT DEPENDABLE STOP SEND MONEY UNDER HEAVY GUARD STOP

Marcus smiled and folded the paper, then slipped it into his pocket.

"That it?" Billy Joe asked.

"Almost," Marcus answered. "Now, all we have to do is wait for the answer he gets back. That way we'll know which train the money will be on."

It was later that same afternoon, when Marcus and the others were eating supper, that they saw the telegrapher come in again. His hair was slicked back, and he was wearing a clean shirt and vest. Marcus could see him standing in the lobby, looking over the assortment of girls who were just beginning to gather there for their evening's work.

"There's Tony," Marcus said.

Tony licked his fingers, then ran them through his hair as he looked over the girls.

"He looks like a fella that's about to sit down to a banquet table, don't he?" Billy Joe said.

"Nothin' will make a man smile like a free trip to the whorehouse," Hank put in.

"Uh, oh, little brother, he's lookin' over toward your girl," Bob teased. By now all of them had seen Loomis and Penny exchange smiles a few times, and they knew he had even visited her once or twice.

Marcus saw Helga come up to greet Tony, then he saw Tony give her a little sheet of yellow paper.

"Hold it, boys," Marcus said. "This might be it."

Helga took the paper and nodded, then Tony pointed to one of the girls. It was the same one Bob had chosen the first day in Ristine. She smiled engagingly at Tony, and the two of them started up the stairs.

"Ha!" Loomis said. "Looks like he went and took your girl instead."

"Looks like it," Bob said.

Helga walked across the dining room, smiling at the other diners, speaking to a group of her girls and some merchants who were eating together before she reached Marcus and his friends.

"Is this what you will be looking for?" she asked.

Marcus opened the page and read the message.

BARLOW GOODWIN

RISTINE, NEVADA

MONEY ON THURSDAY TRAIN STOP SIX GUARDS WITH MONEY SHIPMENT STOP

Marcus read the passage aloud, then smiled.

"Six guards, Marcus. Is not that dangerous?" Helga asked.

"We've took trains with more guards than that, Bob said.

"Yeah," Loomis put in. "With Marcus leadin' us, we could take that train if they had sixteen guards."

"I just hope you know what you be doin'," Helga said.

"Don't you worry none about us, Sugar," Marcus said. "You just keep quiet about what you know, and everything's gonna work out all right."

CHAPTER THIRTEEN

A COLD RAIN BEGAN BEFORE DAWN, AND IT CONTINUED
to slash down on the little town of Ristine. The town
was dark. Most people were still in their beds.

The Grand Hotel was the only exception. A couple
of windows shed light upstairs, while downstairs, in
the back of the hotel, the kitchen was light, and a fire
was set in the cookstove. Atop the stove, a large pot of
coffee perked and simmered, permeating the air with
its bracing aroma.

The back door of the hotel opened, then slammed
shut as Loomis started through the dark and the rain to
the stable which stood some thirty yards distant from
the main building. He hurried across the distance and
slipped into the barn. There, he removed a match from
a waxed, waterproof box and lit a kerosene lantern.
When the flame was turned up, a small golden bubble
of light cast long shadows inside and caused the horses

to move to the front of their stalls, curious as to the intrusion.

"Only me," Loomis said. "I come to check up on you. We'll be ridin' outta here soon's we've had a little breakfast."

Loomis walked over to his horse and stroked its neck. It was dry inside the barn, though the sounds of wind and rain outside were testimony of the wet beginning of the new day. Loomis liked being in a barn under such conditions. He liked the bouquet of leather and wood, the smell of horseflesh, and the aroma of hay.

"You better eat somethin' yourselves," he said, scooping oats into the trough. He continued to talk to the horses as if they could understand him. In fact, Loomis had such a way with them that the others believed he really could speak with them.

Loomis finished feeding them; then he left the barn and hurried through the rain to return to the house.

The others were downstairs in the kitchen now, their saddlebags packed and lying beside the door. All were wearing hats, and though they hadn't yet put on their slickers, they were out and draped across the chairs.

Marcus and Hank were standing by the sideboard drinking coffee. Bob was sitting at the table rolling himself a cigarette. Billy Joe was at the stove, where Helga was frying bacon and eggs in a large, black-iron skillet.

Billy Joe saw a pan of biscuits, golden brown and fluffy, sitting on the edge of the stove. He reached to pick one up, but Helga, muttering in a language that none of them could understand, slapped Billy Joe's hand.

Penny came into the kitchen then. She hadn't dressed but was wearing a robe. She smiled at Loomis

and brushed her hand through her hair.

"You have to leave so early in the morning?" she asked.

"We want to be to the pass well before the train gets there," Marcus said. "We'll have a few things to take care of."

"Speakin' of taking care," Penny said, putting her hand on Loomis's arm. "Will you boys look out for this one?"

"We always do," Hank said.

"The town's beholdin' to you," Penny went on. "Most of the folks got their money back."

"And they still have their land," Marcus said.

"For all the good it's going to do without the railroad," Penny said.

Helga started serving the bacon and eggs then, and Marcus sat down to the table before he answered her.

"I don't claim to know much about it, but seems to me like this here town of Ristine is already goin'. Railroad can't make money without people. If this is where the people are, this is where the railroad's gonna come ... no matter what Goodwin has in mind."

Penny smiled. "Hope so."

"Billy Joe," Helga said after giving him seconds on eggs. "This thing you must do, when finished you be, you will come back to Helga?"

Billy Joe sopped the yellow up with a biscuit. He was quiet for a long moment as if trying to formulate the words. Finally, Helga spoke again.

"Is all right, you do not have to speak," she said. She put her hand on Billy Joe's shoulder. "For Helga, it is careful you will be."

Billy Joe nodded.

Helga left the kitchen then, and for a moment there was an awkward silence.

"You mustn't blame her for speaking what she felt in her heart, Billy Joe," Penny said. "I'll explain it to her after you have gone."

"Thanks," Billy Joe said.

For the next few minutes, the only sound was the scraping of forks on plates and the snapping and popping of the fire in the cook stove. Finally, Marcus stood up and looked at the others.

"All right, boys, get your slickers on. We're about to get wet."

The rain gushed down as they rode. It slashed onto them in stinging sheets and ran in cold rivulets off the folds and creases of their ponchos. It blew in gusts across the trail in front of them and drummed wickedly into the rocks and trees around them. A long, jagged streak of lightning split the dark sky, and for just an instant, the rugged terrain around them was brightly illuminated.

They rode for just over an hour, finally reaching their destination, the pass through which the train would have to come. It was a long, narrow, twisting canyon filled with rocks which had tumbled down from the steep walls and cut with cross ravines and gullies which were bridged by the railroad but which made transit on horseback difficult. The fact that it was dark and storming made it even more difficult, so when halfway through the canyon the rain showed signs of letting up, and the sky grew pale in the east, Marcus was more than a little relieved. Finally they dismounted, then ground-staked their horses.

"All right," Marcus said. "Soon's it's a little more light, let's get some rocks piled up on the track. We get the train stopped, it'll be a lot easier."

"We goin' down there on foot?" Loomis asked.

"Yeah. The footing down there's pretty bad. We don't want to take a chance on havin' one of the horses break a leg. We'll set up an ambush, get the money, come back here, and ride. The folks on the train will be afoot, too."

"I guess you're right," Loomis said.

"Marcus, it's light enough now I can see all the way down to where the track comes into the canyon," Hank said.

"Let's go to work."

At the very moment the boys started building the

barricade on the tracks at the pass, Barlow Goodwin and four of his most trusted commissioners were going into the Grand Hotel. Though dawn had broken, it was still early morning to the residents of the hotel. Most of the girls had worked until the small hours of the morning, and it was normal for them to sleep until noon. Penny and Helga were now back in bed.

Though a desk clerk was officially on duty, so little business came in the morning that he generally slept as late as the girls. Goodwin knew all that and had planned this little morning visit because of it.

As the five men walked across the lobby, guns drawn, one of them stepped on a loose board. It let out a loud creak, and Goodwin held up his hand. Everyone froze in their tracks.

"Shhh!" Goodwin hissed. "If we're gonna do this, we're gonna do it quiet!"

From behind the desk, they could hear the soft, rhythmic snores of the clerk. Goodwin kept them still for a moment longer, listening to the sounds of the hotel. When it was quiet again, he motioned for the men to follow him.

"They're upstairs," he said. "Rooms six, seven, and eight."

"Which ones in which room?" Tanner asked.

"It don't matter. We're gonna kill 'em all," Goodwin said.

Looking like apparitions moving silently through the morning gloom, the men climbed the carpeted stairs to the second floor. Once they reached the second floor landing, they stopped and listened. The entire floor was a symphony of snores and loud, even breathing.

"Which way?" Tanner asked, indicating the U shape of the upper floor.

"This way," Goodwin said, leading them down the right wing.

Slowly, the men continued to creep down the carpeted hallway until they reached the row of three brown-painted doors with little metal numbers indicating six, seven, and eight. Goodwin put two men outside room six, two outside room seven, while he took room eight.

"Get ready," he hissed, and the men raised and cocked their pistols.

Goodwin lifted his leg, and at least one man in front of the other two doors did the same.

"Now!" Goodwin shouted, and he kicked the door open in front of him. With a crashing, smashing noise, the other two doors were kicked open as well.

Goodwin began firing toward the bed, pulling the trigger over and over again as rapidly as he could. After the second discharge, so much smoke had billowed out from the end of his pistol that he couldn't even see the bed but he knew where it was, so he kept firing.

The sudden and sustained firing awakened the entire hotel, and several of the girls screamed. Every man emptied his pistol, shooting six bullets apiece, so that the smoke from thirty shots filled the upstairs hall so thickly that some of the girls and one or two of the men who had paid for the privilege of spending the entire night thought the hotel had caught fire.

Finally, when the last shot was fired, Goodwin and the others stood there waiting for the smoke to clear away.

"Anyone hit?" Goodwin asked.

"Not here."

"Not here, either."

Goodwin smiled. "We got 'em!" he said, enthusiastically. "We caught 'em with their pants down. They didn't even get a chance to get off a shot."

The five men stood there, coughing and gagging in the heavy cordite smoke, waving at it with their hands, trying to make it go away. Finally enough of the smoke had cleared for Goodwin to see the bed. He stared, expecting to see one or two of Quinn's men in there, dead from gunshot wounds. But, as it cleared, he gasped in surprise.

What the hell! he shouted. They's no one in here!"

"Not here, neither."

"This one's empty, too!"

Cursing loudly, Goodwin walked down the rest of the hallway, kicking in the doors. In most rooms he saw only terrified girls. Some rooms were empty, the girls having left when they thought the hotel was afire, and some rooms had men with the girls, merchants and businessmen from the town who were hastily dressing and terrified at the intrusion and the gunplay.

"Where are they?" Goodwin shouted. "Goddamnit! Where are they?"

Penny, who had hoped to stay in her room until Goodwin left, finally realized that she had no choice but to go out into the hall and confront Goodwin. She had one of the few doors left that hadn't been smashed in, and she opened it and stepped outside.

"Mr. Goodwin, what are you doing here smashing up the hotel and terrorizing the other girls?"

"You," Goodwin said, pointing to her. "Where did Quinn and the others go?"

"I don't know."

Goodwin slapped her hard, and Penny's head snapped back. A trickle of blood oozed down from the comer of her mouth.

"Goddamnit! Tell me where they are!"

"I don't know!" Penny said again.

Goodwin drew back his hand to hit her a second time when he was interrupted by a shout from Tanner.

"Hey, Mr. Goodwin, lookee here what I done found in one of their rooms," he said. He came toward Goodwin holding out a little yellow sheet of paper.

"What's that?"

"It's a telegram," Tanner said. "Only thing is, it's to you."

Goodwin took the telegram from Tanner and read

it. It was the one telling him that the money would be sent.

"Sonofabitch!" he swore. "Those bastards are plannin' to hold up the train. Come on, we've got to stop them."

"Uh, Mr. Goodwin, don't you think we ought to get some help?" Tanner asked.

"Help? We didn't need no help when we come in here this mornin', did we?"

"That was different," Tanner said. "We figured they'd be asleep in their beds. It's easy enough to kill a man while he's asleep. But don't forget, I seen that Quinn fella shoot down Eugene when Eugene had the drop on him."

Goodwin stroked his chin for a moment, then looked at Penny. He smiled evilly. "All right, then we'll take somethin' along to give us an edge. Get your clothes on," he said to Penny. "You're goin' with us."

Back in the canyon, Quinn's Raiders were ready. A barricade of stone had been built on the track, and every man had found a position which would give them a field of fire toward the train while offering some protection from return fire. The train entered the pass from the far end, puffing loudly; the puffs of steam were picked up by the walls of the canyon and reverberated back in booming echoes.

"Get ready! Here it comes!" Marcus shouted.

They waited for several anxious moments until they were sure the engineer had seen the barricade. They heard him throw on his brakes, heard the terrible screech of steel on steel as the train finally slid to a halt. By now, just as they had calculated, the train was right below them.

The door to the baggage car opened, and two armed men jumped down onto the berm alongside the track. One of them stood just outside the car looking around, while the other started up toward the engine.

"What is it? Why'd you stop in here?" Marcus heard the man asked.

"Didn't have no choice," the engineer said, climbing down the side of his engine. "Look at them rocks."

"Up there!" the man on the ground beside the baggage car suddenly shouted, pointing to the rocks where Marcus and Billy Joe had taken cover.

"Damn, I have to give it to the sonofabitch, he knows his job," Marcus said. "Billy Joe, keep the engineer from getting back into the train, else he'll back it out of here."

"Right," Billy Joe answered, and he fired his Mare's Leg, the heavy-caliber gun he carried, at the engine cab just as the engineer started to climb up. It put a dent the size of a man's fist in the heavy iron sheathing of the engine. That was enough to cause the engineer to abandon the engine and run for cover in the rocks alongside.

Two more guards came out of the baggage car and began shooting up toward them. Two more started firing from farther back on the train. It was a little like popcorn popping in a pan, starting slow and building to a crescendo, with so many of the kernels popping at once that the individual pops couldn't be discerned.

The shooting was like that now as gunfire rang from the canyon walls and from the train.

Bullets fried the air beside them, hit the rocks, and whined off into the distance. Some of the closer misses sent chips of rock dust into Marcus's face, stinging him with its spray.

One of the guards from the back of the train was hit, and he fell to the ground, sliding face down to the bottom of the ballast-covered berm. The guard who had gone forward to question the engineer was down, and with a well-aimed shot, Marcus took out the one that was on the ground in front of the baggage car.

Marcus looked toward the back of the train and he saw Loomis drop from the canyon wall onto the top of the rear passenger car. Loomis had put his pistol in his holster and was carrying a knife. Marcus also saw one of the train guards climbing up the ladder at the back of the same car. Marcus tried to shoot the guard off, but he moved around behind the car too fast.

"Loomis!" he shouted. "Behind you!"

Because of the noise of the gunfire, Loomis didn't hear the warning. In another minute the guard would have an easy shot at Loomis's back.

Marcus shot at the car, ricochetting his bullet off just in front of Loomis. Startled, Loomis looked over toward Marcus. Marcus pointed to the rear of the car.

Loomis turned just as the guard reached the top. With a quick, deft move, Loomis threw his knife, and Marcus saw the blade bury itself deep into the guard's chest. The guard pitched off the car and landed on the track behind, dead. Loomis turned and waved at Marcus, then, pulling his pistol, ran forward toward the baggage car.

Hank was next to drop down onto the train and he, carrying a sawed-off shotgun, and Loomis, with his pistol in his hand, moved forward to the baggage car. By now, the only return fire was coming from inside the car.

"Come on out!" Marcus called. "You're all that's left."

"We ain't comin' out!" The guard punctuated his statement with two quick shots.

"Billy Joe, shoot out that damn window," Marcus said, pointing to a small window at the top of the car.

Billy Joe shot the window with his Mare's Leg, and the window, frame and all, was torn away.

"You men have five seconds to come out!" Marcus called. "If you don't, we're gonna put dynamite in through that window."

"How you gonna get it in?" one of the guards called back.

"Show 'em, Hank," Marcus called.

Hank, who was on top of the car now, lay down on his stomach and stuck the barrel of his shotgun through the window. He let go a blast.

"We're comin' out! Don't shoot no more, an' don't throw no dynamite in here!"

Marcus, Billy Joe, and Bob covered the baggage car from outside, while Loomis and Hank covered it from the top. The doors slid open, and two men hopped down. One was holding his arm, the other was peppered with shot, probably ricochets from Hank's blast. He wasn't very badly hurt, and he was carrying a canvas bag with a leather strap.

"There's five thousand dollars in here," he said, tossing the bag to Marcus. "I reckon this is what you're after."

Marcus smiled. "I reckon it is," he said. He nodded toward one of the guards on the ground. The guard was moving, indicating that he was still alive. "Get your dead and wounded back on the train. Engineer!"

"Yes, sir," the engineer answered nervously from his position behind a nearby rock.

"When ever'one's on board, you back the train out of this canyon. Give us an hour to get away, then you can come back in and take down the barricade."

"Yes, sir," the engineer said. He started toward the engine.

Marcus, Billy Joe, and Bob left on one side of the train, while Loomis and Hank left on the other. That was to confuse the witnesses so that they wouldn't be able to tell whether the robbers left to the north or the south. Ten minutes later, all five met up again, then went to reclaim their horses.

"I believe this one went off slicker'n any we ever pulled," Bob said. "Yes, sir, Marcus, you had this one planned right down to the last—"

"Loomis! Goodwin's here! He's going to... ." the shout came from Penny, but that was as far as she got. Her warning was cut off by a pistol shot.

The boys saw Penny fall and also saw a little puff of smoke drifting away from an outcropping of rocks just behind her.

"Get down!" Marcus shouted, and the Raiders dropped to the ground, though there was very little for cover.

Bullets whizzed and popped all around them, and Marcus and the others were in the uncomfortable position of behind exposed. They had to roll from one place to another, trying to find shelter behind rocks that were too small for the job. On the other hand, Goodwin and his men were in excellent position.

Marcus fired in the direction where the shots were coming from, and he watched his bullets chip away rock, but he knew he wasn't doing any good.

"Penny?" Marcus called. "Penny? Can you move?"

"She can't move, Quinn, 'cause she's dead," Goodwin called back. He laughed.

"You didn't have to kill her, you sonofabitch."

"What's one less whore?" Goodwin said. "There'll be another to take her place tomorrow."

"You'll never know about it," Quinn said.

"Yeah? You're the one out in the open," Goodwin

shouted. Goodwin and his men fired again, and the bullets hit the rocks all around Marcus, rattling like hail.

"Hank," Marcus called, quietly. "I'm going to move forward. When I give you the word, all of you give me as much covering fire as you can."

"Right," Hank answered.

Marcus breathed deeply several times, then looked over at Hank and nodded. The Raiders began a sustained firing toward the rocks where Goodwin and his men were. Marcus got up and ran forward several feet, then dived for the cover behind a large rock. He skinned his elbow and barked his knees, but he managed to slide in behind the rock.

"Where the hell did Quinn go?" Marcus heard Goodwin say. Marcus smiled. The firing had kept their heads down so well that they hadn't even seen him move.

Marcus started to plan his next rush when he happened to notice that a long, low ridge might conceal him long enough to allow him to crawl over to the same rock formation Goodwin had. He would have to wriggle on his belly to stay low enough.

Hank and Bob opened fire, while Loomis and Billy Joe fell back. Then Billy Joe and Loomis provided covering fire for Hank and Bob to withdraw.

"Pretty good, Quinn," Goodwin called. "I didn't see you get back there. It ain't gonna do you no good."

"They got more cover now," Marcus heard Tanner say.

"Don't worry about it," Goodwin answered. "They can't get to their horses, and they can't get to water. We can just wait 'em out."

Marcus started crawling on his belly, protected by the long, low spine of rock that jutted out from a larger section of boulders. Once, he dislodged a rock, and he stopped and held his breath.

"I heard somethin'."

"Probably a rabbit or somethin'. Just keep your eyes on them rocks over there. They can't move without us seein' them."

Taking a deep breath, Marcus crawled several more feet. There was another brisk exchange of gunfire, and Marcus used that to cover his last fifteen feet. Finally he made it to the cover of some large boulders. He moved around behind them, then climbed up the back side. Three minutes later he was on top of the outcropping, looking right down onto Goodwin and the men with him. There were five, and they all had their backs turned to him. He checked his load to make sure he had enough bullets in the cylinder, then he stood up and aimed down at them.

"All right, drop your guns, all of you," he said quietly.

"What the hell?" Gilmore shouted, and he spun quickly, raising his pistol and firing as he did so. Marcus returned fire, and Gilmore grabbed at his chest, then fell back against the rocks. No one else fired, but all still held their guns.

"Now he's gonna die slow and painful," Marcus said. "Who's gonna be next?"

"Not me," Tanner said, throwing his gun down.

"Me neither."

"You yellow bastards!" Goodwin shouted. "There's only one of him."

"You can have him all to yourself," the last commissioner said, and he dropped his pistol, too.

Now it was between the two armed men, while three more stood aside, their guns on the ground, their arms raised. A fourth was sitting against a rock, his head tossed back, his eyes closed tightly, totally uninterested in what was happening around him. He was dying with a bullet in his lungs.

"Hank!" Marcus shouted. "Come on, I got them."

"I guess you have at that," Goodwin said, putting his gun down. He raised his arms; then he smiled. "The question is, what are you going to do with us? You can't turn us over to the law. I am the law."

"Wrong," Marcus said. "I just tried you for Penny's murder."

"What?"

"I find you guilty and sentence you to die," Marcus said. He leveled his pistol at Goodwin's face.

"No, you can't do that!" Goodwin shouted, thrusting both hands out in front of him, as if in that way he could stop the bullet. Marcus fired, and his bullet clipped off the end of one of Goodwin's fingers before it hit him right between the eyes. He was slammed back against the rock, then bounced forward, landing belly down. A pool of blood began to spread from under his head.

"Wrong again, you sonofabitch," Marcus said, even as the echo of the last shot was still reverberating in the hills.

Loomis brought the horses over then, and Quinn and the others mounted up. Tanner and the two surviving commissioners were still standing with their arms raised.

"You gonna kill us, too?" Tanner asked.

Marcus adjusted his hat slowly and looked down at the man. "Hell, you boys ain't worth good lead. Just see you bury Penny back at Ristine."

The frightened men still held their hands high as they watched Quinn's Raiders ride out of the canyon.

T*he End.*

A LOOK AT: LONG ROAD TO ABILENE, THE WESTERN ADVENTURES OF CADE MCCALL BOOK I

LONG ROAD TO ABILENE, is a classic hero's journey, a western adventure that exemplifies the struggles, the defeats, and the victories that personify the history of the American West. After surviving the bloody battle of Franklin and the hell of a Yankee prison camp, Cade McCall comes home to the woman he loves only to find that she, believing him dead, has married his brother. With nothing left to keep him in Tennessee, Cade journeys to New Orleans where an encounter with a beautiful woman leads to being shanghaied for an unexpected adventure at sea. Returning to Texas, he signs on to drive a herd of cattle to Abilene, where he is drawn into a classic showdown of good versus evil, and a surprising reunion with an old enemy.

AVAILABLE NOW FROM ROBERT VAUGHAN AND WOLFPACK PUBLISHING.

ABOUT THE AUTHOR

Robert Vaughan sold his first book when he was 19. That was 57 years and nearly 500 books ago. He wrote the novelization for the miniseries *Andersonville*. Vaughan wrote, produced, and appeared in the History Channel documentary *Vietnam Homecoming*. His books have hit the NYT bestseller list seven times. He has won the Spur Award, the PORGIE Award (Best Paperback Original), the Western Fictioneers Lifetime Achievement Award, received the Readwest President's Award for Excellence in Western Fiction, is a member of the American Writers Hall of Fame and is a Pulitzer Prize nominee. Vaughn is also a retired army officer, helicopter pilot with three tours in Vietnam. And received the Distinguished Flying Cross, the Purple Heart, The Bronze Star with three oak leaf clusters, the Air Medal for valor with 35 oak leaf clusters, the Army Commendation Medal, the Meritorious Service Medal, and the Vietnamese Cross of Gallantry.

Made in the USA
Coppell, TX
06 December 2022

88026391R00132